Contents

Jean Ure

Plague

Previously published as *Plague 99*

mammoth

First published in Great Britain 1989
by Methuen Children's Books Ltd
as *Plague 99*
Published 1991 by Mammoth
Reissued 1999 by Mammoth
an imprint of Egmont Children's Books Limited
239 Kensington High Street, London W8 6SA

Text copyright © 1989 Jean Ure
Cover illustration copyright © 1999 Lee Gibbons

The moral rights of the author and illustrator have been asserted.

ISBN 0 7497 0333 4

1 3 5 7 9 10 8 6 4 2

A CIP catalogue record for this title
is available from the British Library

Printed in Great Britain
by Cox & Wyman Ltd, Reading, Berkshire

'It's been a bit like the Stone Age, I suppose, really.'

Four weeks completely shut away from the rest of humanity. Living on orange juice and apples, on lentils and beans and potatoes in their jackets: on porridge made with soya milk, and vegetable hot pot. No newspapers, no television; no radio, no mail. Isolated.

There were fourteen of them in all – six boys, six girls, plus Rod and Sarah, the two leaders. Rod and Sarah had said from the beginning that they were to be called by their first names. Fran had found it quite difficult, to start with. After all, they were so much older than the rest of them. Harry would have tossed her head and said, 'So what?' She wouldn't have had any difficulty; she never did. It always took Fran more time to accustom herself to new ways than it did Harry. While Harry, for instance, had adapted to the perils of a large comprehensive (after a small church primary) almost overnight, Fran had been fretted and bothered for the whole of their first term. Even now, all these years later, she sometimes wasn't really sure that she felt part of the community. Without Harry she doubted if she would ever have survived. Without Harry she almost *hadn't* survived the four weeks of camp. She almost hadn't come.

It had been Harry's idea, of course; most things were.

'Look!' she had cried, dragging Fran the length of the school corridor to the notice-board in the main hall. '*We* could go on that!'

Fran had stared, doubtfully, at a large notice which said,

SIXTH FORMERS! SICK OF SOFT OPTIONS? THEN COME AND PROVE YOURSELVES! CAN *YOU* EXIST

FOR FOUR WEEKS WITHOUT THE BENEFITS OF CIVILISATION?

Fran on her own would not have been at all sure that she wanted to: Fran with Harry could see that it might be fun. Four weeks away from towns and traffic and the stink of diesel . . .

And then, after all, Harry had been unable to come. Two days before they were due to leave she had fallen out of her shoes, coming down the stairs ('Heels six inches high! I *told* you not to wear them'), and been taken to the casualty department with a broken wrist. It seemed there could be no question of a person existing for four weeks without the benefits of civilisation with a broken wrist. The doctor wouldn't hear of it; nor would Harry's mum, even though she wasn't the fussing type. Harry, her wrist enclosed in a plaster tube, her arm held up in a sling, had wailed tragically.

'This is disaster! You'll go off and lose *pounds*. You'll come back all gorgeous and gaunt and I'll still be stuck here with my flab!'

Harry actually hadn't any flab. She was tiny and dark, like her mother, and was going to specialise in physical training. It was Fran, the artist, the dreamer, the sitter-about-doing-seemingly-nothing, and built on more statuesque lines to begin with, who could do with shedding a few pounds. But hopefully, trying to sound self-sacrificing, she'd suggested, 'Maybe I shouldn't go, either?'

'Of course you must go!' had said Harry's mum.

'I think you ought,' had said Fran's.

Fran's dad had been the only one to support her. He hadn't been all that keen on the idea to start with – a bit of a worrier was Fran's dad. Fran sometimes thought that she took after him. Her mum only worried that at the age of sixteen Fran had never yet been away from home by herself. Truth to tell, it worried Fran a bit, too. Was it right, at sixteen, never to have slept away from her parents for one single night? (Except for the times she had slept round at

2

Harry's, but that didn't count: she and Harry had been best mates since kindergarten.)

'You can't back out at this stage,' Fran's mum had said. 'It wouldn't be fair; not both of you.'

In fact there had been a whole long list of people wanting to go off and prove themselves; their places could easily have been filled even at this late hour – as indeed Harry's was. Fran's mum knew it as well as Fran. What she was really saying was, 'I think it would be good for you.'

A small, reluctant part of Fran had agreed with her: a much larger part of Fran had been thrown into panic. Her dad, protective, seeing her off at the station on the Monday morning, had made her promise to 'Let us know immediately if you want to come home'.

Fran's mum had said, 'She won't want to come home! She'll enjoy herself once she's there.'

'And anyway,' Fran had said, trying to make light of it but not quite able to keep the wobble from her voice, 'we can't write or telephone.'

'You'd have to, my lass, if there was an emergency!'

'There won't be any emergency.' Fran's mum had been brisk and cheerful; determined to show that *she* had no doubts. But at the last minute she had hugged Fran and whispered, 'Be brave! Four weeks isn't that long. It'll pass far quicker than you think.'

It hadn't seemed, at the beginning, as if it would ever pass at all. All about her there had been people having fun – laughing, joking, forming relationships – and Fran in their midst, an awkward stranger. With Harry she could have found the courage to unbend and join in: without Harry, she was nothing. She was nobody. It was everything she had most dreaded. Fran-on-her-own, paralysed with fright: Fran-away-from-home, unable to function. But she had stuck it out; she had survived. The month hadn't exactly passed quickly – but it had passed. Some of it, towards the end, she had even started to enjoy. She knew that at heart she was still what her mum called a 'home body' – not bold

3

or adventurous, certainly not the stuff from which heroines are made; but for all that, she had done it. And now –

'Let's have a song!' called Sarah. 'A Stone Age song ... come along, folks! Ging gang gooly gooly gooly gooly *wotcha* –'

'Ging gan goo, ging gang goo!' Fran joined in with the others. The month had passed – and tomorrow she was going back home!

Sajjad Khan lay on his bed asking for water. There wasn't any, until Shahid had boiled some, and then it would take for ever to cool. He had had a big pan standing ready on the stove all day. All he had to do was put a light under it. No big deal. Just go into the kitchen and turn on the gas. Instead, he had spent the entire day slumped before the television, watching reruns of old movies, which was all they now seemed to be showing. Occasionally there had been a bit of news, the usual bland assurances by so-called experts: 'There is no need for panic: the situation is under control.' Shahid didn't believe a word of it.

He had roused himself just once during the course of the day, to go to the bathroom and look in on his father on the way back. The old man had been unconscious, and even if he hadn't been there was nothing anyone could do for him. There wasn't anyone around to do anything for anyone.

Shahid had stayed just long enough to check he wasn't actually dead and had gone back to the television. They were showing a film called *Casablanca*. He'd heard of *Casablanca*; it was one of those cult movies it was smart to have seen at least a dozen times. It was the first time Shahid had seen it. He found it disappointing. It struck him as what Mr Smithers at school would have called banal (pronounced bay-nal, because that was Mr Smithers for you). He'd have switched to another channel if he could have summoned up the energy. He couldn't be bothered. Like he couldn't be bothered to go through into the kitchen and turn on the gas and open a can of whatever there was. There

4

weren't many cans left now. His mother hadn't believed in convenience food – well, she might have done, given half a chance, but his old man would never have allowed it, just as he hadn't allowed a whole heap of other things. Boyfriends, girlfriends, mixed bathing, school plays, youth club, disco . . . the list was endless. The Führer was how Shahid referred to him behind his back. The little tinpot Führer, doing his bits, exercising his petty power, tyrannising over them all. And now he lay there, bleating for water.

Shahid stood in the bedroom doorway, staring unmoved at his father on the bed. It would be at least an hour before the large pan had boiled and the water cooled sufficiently to be drinkable. He didn't know why he kept on bothering with all this boiling crap anyway. He only did it because *they* said you ought, but they said a whole load of things that nobody took any notice of. Disposal of rubbish, disposal of bodies. Some things just weren't practical. Others – well, others were so obviously just said as a sop to keep the populace from going bananas. 'Only travel if your journey is strictly necessary. Try to use private transport wherever possible.' Private transport! That was a joke (unless they meant feet). Public transport was even more of a joke. Try finding any. Even just travelling was a bit of a laugh. Travel to where? And for what purpose? They must think people were complete idiots.

Why didn't he put the *kettle* on and boil that?

He hadn't put it on before because he hadn't thought of it.

And he wasn't putting it on now because he couldn't be bothered.

That was the simple truth: he just couldn't be bothered.

The thing on the bed was still moaning. The thing was his father. He must remember: *this is your father*. His father wanted water. Any water would do. Why keep the thing (his father) in torment when it was going to die very soon whether the water was boiled or whether it wasn't?

Shahid peeled himself away from the door and lurched, zombie-like, along the narrow passage to the small kitchen, which looked across to the identical small kitchen of the

5

identical flat in the identical block opposite. Up until a few days ago he had seen the family who lived there, moving about, preparing food, boiling water. The last person he had seen was the youngest child, in its nappy, standing up on the draining-board, fiddling with the window. Fortunately the locks were all child-proof. Shahid had stayed watching for a while, until the child had either grown bored or decided there must be easier ways of committing suicide and gone crawling off to investigate. He hadn't seen it again, nor any of the rest of the family.

He filled a glass at the cold tap, probably all full of cholera bugs, or typhoid: they were obviously terrified of starting an epidemic (ho ho, what a laugh) which was why they had said to boil the stuff, but circumstances alter cases as somebody or other had once memorably decreed. If a person were going to die within the next forty-eight hours it wouldn't really seem to matter very much if they drank a glass full of cholera bugs before they went.

Carefully, inserting his hands into the ballooning membranes that had once been rubber gloves – they had been soaked so many times in bleach they were probably porous – he carried the glass of bugs back along the passage to his parents' bedroom. On the way he passed the closed door of what had been his sisters' and grandmother's room. He had opened the windows as wide as they would go, and drawn the curtains against the sun, and even stuffed a rug along the bottom of the door, but by some process of osmosis – osmosis? Was that the word? Well, anyway, by some process the smell had leaked out and was beginning to pervade the rest of the flat. All very well them talking about polythene bags and digging trenches. It was like telling people to hide under the dining-room table in the event of nuclear war. It just wasn't feasible. Not if you lived eight floors up and were entirely surrounded by concrete, and anyway, where were you supposed to get polythene bags from? Of *that* size and strength? He'd like to see one of them trying to shovel bits and pieces into a dustbin liner.

Shahid felt suddenly sick. He pressed a gloved hand to his

mask, trying to force back the tidal waves of nausea. The worst was yet to come. Water the thing and *then* be sick.

Sajjad Khan had entered the final phase. Shahid didn't look as he held the glass of water to the swollen lips. He kept his eyes on the sky and his thoughts on birds and flowers, and the scent that the senior art mistress at school, Mrs Penny, used to wear. Shahid, being awkward and left-handed and artistically null and void, had never had any classes with Mrs Penny; but everyone knew her scent as she swept through the school corridors. Dior it was, according to Julie.

'Her boyfriend brought it back from Paris.'

Julie and Shahid had talked of going to Paris. It had been only a pipe dream, of course; his father would have seen to that.

He left the glass on the table by the side of the bed. All the change from his father's pocket was there, along with his reading glasses and a pile of cards advertising the Taj Mahal Indian restaurant. They were new cards, embossed in red, to go with the new red wallpaper and wine-coloured carpet. There was a whole unopened box of them in the hall. Shahid was supposed to have been scattering them round the area, pushing them through doorways. Even as short a while as a fortnight ago his father had been nagging him about it.

'Did you send out those cards yet?'

In the middle of a nuclear holocaust he would have nagged about his cards.

Back in the sitting room the television was showing *The Magnificent Seven*. Shahid practically knew *The Magnificent Seven* off by heart: he had already seen it three times.

Pulling up a chair, he settled down to see it yet again.

2

'Are we all gathered?' Rod turned, to count heads, 'Right, then, let's be making tracks!'

It was Sunday morning. Camp had been struck, everything made good: rubbish buried, bothies dismantled, latrines filled in. The ashes of the fire had been raked over, the area covered with fresh-cut turf. Now they were setting off down the lane – that same lane which four weeks ago Fran had trodden on leaden foot, dreading what was to come – back to civilisation.

Perversely, while still yearning for home and for her parents, Fran found that now the time had come she was almost sorry to be leaving. The others spoke longingly of baths and hot dinners – 'Roast beef! Yum yum!' Some of the girls couldn't wait to catch up on the latest episodes of *Families*. While Fran agreed that a real bath would be pleasant (though a dip in the stream on a hot day had been more refreshing than any bath could ever be), she didn't care over much about the hot dinners, she didn't think she would ever go back to eating meat again, and the only reason she watched *Families* was to keep up with Harry. Harry was an addict: she watched all the soaps. Fran was more often shut away in her room, drawing or painting. Harry had once accused her, only half-jokingly, of being nun-like. Mr Smithers at school called her a technophobe – 'Show Fran a microchip and she goes all to pieces! You'd have done better in the days of horse-drawn carriages.'

There were times when Fran thought that he might be right. She listened to her parents' tales of steam trains, of butchers' boys on bicycles, and big liners like the Queen

Mary stately sailing the Atlantic, and she felt a strong sense of nostalgia for an age which she had never known.

'Things went on for years, then, just the same.'

That would have suited Fran: she hated change and turmoil.

'This is it, folks!' Sarah hauled at the straps of her haversack, hoisting it more securely on to her back. 'The moment of truth!'

They had reached the end of the lane. They turned the corner, up the rutted track leading to the ruined church with its abandoned churchyard where they had been allowed to park. There was Rod's old transit van with Sarah's mini, side by side beneath the yew tree, just as they had left them. They stood for a second, drinking in the silence. A wood pigeon cooed somewhere overhead, a squirrel chattered at the base of the tree; otherwise, nothing. Nothing and no one.

'So what did we expect?' Rod gave a little laugh. Rueful, self-mocking. 'A reception committee?'

Well, yes, if the truth were known they probably had. And why not? It wasn't every day that people went off to live without the benefits of civilisation for a whole month. Before they set out the local radio and television stations had seemed quite interested. They had wanted all the details – how many people were going, how old they were, which schools they were from – they had even made a note of the time at which they were due to break camp. Sarah, looking at her watch, said, 'Nine o'clock. Is that what we told them?'

'Between eight-thirty and nine.'

'So maybe we should hang on a bit, just in case?'

'We'll give them ten minutes. Let's get the gear stashed.'

By quarter-past nine nobody had turned up and Rod was impatient to be moving. It was a bit of an anticlimax – even Fran had been looking forward to seeing herself on television – but as Rod said, trying to put a brave face on things, it just went to show that you were never as important as you thought you were.

'Come on, then, the people who are with me!' Sarah wrenched open the door of her mini. 'Let's move it.'

Two of the boys and one of the girls climbed into the mini, the rest piled into the van, with its message, MEAT MEANS MURDER: POWER IS POLLUTION, painted on the side in bright green letters.

'OK?' said Rod. 'London here we come!'

They were going back cross-country, bypassing Derby, to pick up the M1. The two vehicles drove in convoy.

'No stopping off,' said Rod, 'save in emergencies.'

Rod had a wife and small baby at home and was eager to get back. So was Fran, now that at last they were under way. She didn't want to hang around, eating sawdust sarnies in motorway caffs. Anyway, the sandwiches wouldn't be vegan and so long as they were with Rod there could be no bending of the rules.

The roads cross-country were surprisingly quiet. What with its being August and the height of the holiday season, not to mention all the normal Sunday diversions and road-works, Rod had estimated it would be a good hour before they hit the motorway; in fact it took them only half that time. Even the M1 itself seemed curiously devoid of traffic.

Steven, one of the boys, said, 'Did you know that in the last twenty miles we've seen only one car?'

'Don't knock it,' said Rod. 'At this rate we'll be home by mid-afternoon!'

'It's weird, though,' said Steven, 'isn't it?'

'Not really. Just nice and quiet.'

Someone said, 'Put the radio on.' Rod laughed. 'You'll be lucky!' The radio in Rod's van emitted nothing but static. It had been the same on the way up. 'No mod cons here, I'm afraid . . . you could always try a tape.'

Groans. 'Not The Smiths again!'

'There should be a Dylan somewhere.'

'Dylan! How old are you, granddad?'

'Thirty-three,' said Rod.

'Man, that is ancient!'

At the turn-off for Luton the cars parted company. Sarah

in her mini was driving straight through to central London, while Rod was dropping one of the girls, Susie, and two of the boys, including Steven, at Luton station to complete their journey by train.

'Wow!' said Steven. 'So this is Luton, folks! Hub of the universe.'

Someone said, 'I always did want to see Luton.'

'Imagine *living* here,' said Susie.

'Does anyone? Or is it just a myth?'

'Looks like a myth to me . . . yell if you see any signs!'

'Some people,' said Rod, 'are just never happy. I get you here forty minutes ahead of schedule – '

'We'll die of boredom!'

'So go for an earlier train, or have a cup of coffee . . . Go on! I never heard such base ingratitude. Out you get!'

Mournfully, Susie shouldered her rucksack. 'If you say, O Master.'

They watched the three of them move off, across the silent street.

Someone said, 'Did you ever see a play called *The Ghost Train*?'

'No. Why?'

'I was just suddenly reminded of it.'

'It's very quiet,' said Fran.

'Yeah . . . maybe World War Three's broken out and we're the only ones that don't know about it.'

That was Will Parker, who had been Steven's friend. They turned on him and yelled.

'*Sick!*'

'I was being serious,' said Will.

'Even sicker!'

'Well, it's bloody odd, though.'

One of the girls leaned forward, anxiously, to Rod. 'You don't think something's happened, do you?'

'Nah! Course not.' Rod swung the wheel round. 'Typical English Sunday.'

'Then w – '

'Button it, Parker! Who's got a song?'

11

By midday they had reached the outskirts of London.

'Home in time for me roast beef and two veg!' cried Will.

'Parker,' said Rod, 'you are being purposely provoking . . . in any case we've got the M25 coming up. That'll put an end to your foul meat-eating intentions.'

One of the girls said, 'D'you remember that tailback on the way out? I thought we'd be stuck there all month.'

'Yes, if we're going to hit trouble,' said Rod, 'this'll be where it's at.'

The M25 was almost empty. Even Rod seemed somewhat shaken.

'This I cannot believe,' he said.

'I told you,' said Will, 'the Third W – '

'Shut up, William! Concentrate on your murdered animal and two veg . . . Fran, I've been wondering. Would it be OK if I ditched you in Purley, rather than going all the way through to Croydon? Would that be OK for you?'

'Yes,' said Fran. 'Purley would be fine.'

'Are you quite sure? I don't want you to feel abandoned. It's just – well! Croydon is a bit out of the way for the rest of us.'

'What he actually means,' said Will, 'is that he has a delectable young wife he can't wait to get back to.'

'And a delectable young baby,' said Rod, amidst laughter. 'Seriously, though, Fran – '

'No, really,' she said. 'Purley is practically on the doorstep.'

That was a bit of an exaggeration, but she could easily catch a bus. She could even walk, if necessary, though it was a fair step with a rucksack. She glanced at her watch. She would be home a good couple of hours before she was expected. Dad would be relieved to see her. She bet he was chewing his nails even now, wondering where she was, worrying about accidents. Mum would be saying, 'Oh, do calm down, you silly man! She can't possibly get here before three o'clock.'

'Now, are you quite certain,' said Rod, 'that this is all right?'

12

Fran said again that it was fine. He seemed to be as great a worrier as her dad. She wouldn't have thought it of Rod.

She waved as the van drove off, and settled down to wait for her bus. After lunch, she thought, she would go round and see Harry. Four weeks was the longest they had ever been apart. They would have so much to tell it would take all the rest of the day.

Come on, bus! She wanted to get home.

There were any number of buses which went from Purley to Croydon; but one had to remember, of course, that it was Sunday. Typical English Sunday. People weren't supposed to travel around and do things on a Sunday. Not in England.

She waited twenty minutes, then decided to walk. It wasn't that far; she would still have time to eat lunch and go round to Harry's.

She toyed for a moment with the idea of finding a telephone box and calling home, but that would only put Dad in one of his states. 'Walk all the way from Purley? In this heat?' He'd start panicking and want to call a cab, which would be ridiculous. If he'd had a car he'd be over in a flash, but the Latimers had never had one, neither Mum nor Dad had ever learnt to drive. They weren't really driving sort of people. And anyway, what were a few paltry miles to one who had existed without the benefits of civilisation for a whole month?

Humping her rucksack on to her back, Fran set off along the main road. If a bus came and she was near a stop she would take it; if not, she would turn off by the Goat and Compasses and go up the hill.

It was as quiet in Purley as it had been everywhere else, but then it was probably always quiet in Purley, on a Sunday. Fran didn't really think anything of it, except that it was pleasant, walking in the sunshine without the usual roar of traffic and accompanying stink of diesel.

She reached the Goat and Compasses at twenty-past one. The chairs and tables were all set out on the patio, only no one was sitting at them, which might have struck her as odd, on a sunny summer's day, if her overwhelming feeling hadn't been one of relief: she hated having to walk past the groups of drinking youths and their girlfriends. (Sometimes it was youths on their own and that was even worse, because then they shouted things and made her blush.)

Up Pearson's Hill she toiled with her rucksack; turned right at the top, along Gibson's Close, past the allotments, down the –

Fran stopped. A barricade of barbed wire was blocking the footpath. It stretched away in a diagonal line, right across the allotments, on to the row of houses in The Mount. She stared, indignantly. They couldn't block the footpath! It was a public right of way. You couldn't go blocking off public rights of way! It was against the law. You had to have an act of parliament. No one, not even the Council –

From behind her, a voice spoke. It was a child's voice. It said: 'You can't get through. We're not allowed.'

Fran sprang round. Two children, a girl and a boy, had crept silently up and were standing side by side solemnly looking at her. The girl, who was the one who had spoken, was about nine or ten, the boy a bit younger. Both were wearing gauze masks, the kind used by surgeons. Playing at doctors, thought Fran.

'What is it?' She gestured, at the barricade.

'It's to stop people,' said the girl.

'Stop people getting in?'

'Stop people getting out.'

'It goes all the way round London.' That was the boy. He held out his arms, in a big circle. 'Right the way round.'

The boy was too young. He didn't know what he was talking about. Fran appealed to the girl. 'Who put it there?'

'They did.'

'Who's they? The Council?'

The girl thought about it. 'The Gov'ment.'

'The Government?'

'It wasn't the Gov'ment. It was soldiers.' That was the boy again. 'Soldiers with guns. Why aren't you wearing your mask?'

'I don't need a mask.' Fran brushed the question aside,

14

impatiently. She didn't feel like playing games. 'You only need a mask if you work in the operating theatre. When did the sold – '

'Everyone has to have a mask.'

'No, they don't! When did – '

'They do, they said.'

'Well, I haven't got one.' If it had really been soldiers that must mean there was something dangerous, like . . . like a bomb. 'Is it a bomb?' she said.

The children stared at her, blankly.

'Is that why they've put the fence there?'

'It's there to stop people.'

'Yes, I know! You told me. But w – '

'No one's allowed to go in, and anyone that's already in's not allowed to come out.'

'Yeah, an' if they do, they shoot them!' The boy sprayed machine-gun bullets. Fran, involuntarily, took a step backwards.

'Who shoots them?'

'The soldiers.'

'Why?'

''Cos they're not allowed!'

'But *why*? *Why* aren't they allowed?'

''Cos if they got out we'd all die.'

'Why haven't you got a mask?' said the girl.

'Because nobody gave me one!' Fran was beginning, now, to feel frightened. 'What do we need masks for?'

'Stop you breathing the germs.'

'What germs?'

The children stood, stolidly regarding her.

'*What germs*?' screamed Fran.

'Germs that come from over there.' The girl raised her arm and pointed across the barricade. 'That's where the germs are. That's why we're not allowed in.'

'But I've got to get in! I live there!' She felt almost desperate enough to hurl her sleeping-bag at the barbed wire and try to take the barricade by storm. 'They can't stop people getting to their homes!'

But they could; if it was an emergency. If it was an emergency they could do whatever they liked.

'Down there – ' the girl turned and pointed back towards the main road ' – there's a bus on its side and all soldiers.'

Fran swallowed. 'You mean . . . it crashed?'

'No. The soldiers put it there.'

'The soldiers put the bus there?'

'So's no one could get through. And now they're guarding it.'

'With guns.'

'Where – ' Fran's voice cracked. She cleared her throat. 'Where is it? The bus?'

'In the main road.'

'But *where*?'

'By the school. Where the park is.'

Fran's last hopes went crashing. She needed to be on the other side of the school if she were to get home. She turned, and ran back again to the barricade. Only a couple of hundred metres! That was all that separated her from Mum and Dad – that and a row of houses. She looked again at the houses. For the first time she realised: they had all been boarded up. Of course they were quite old: Victorian, Edwardian. Mum had always hated them. Said it was about time they came down. Mum . . . oh, Mum! Where are you?

Something plucked at her sleeve. It was the boy.

'I know a way you can get in.'

Fran dug her knuckles into the hollows beneath her eyes. 'How?'

'In that house over there.' He pointed. 'You can go down the steps and get out the other side.'

'You mean . . . through the basement?'

'It's easy. There's a little window.'

'How do you know?' The girl had turned on him. Her voice was high and agitated, her eyes above the mask sharp with sudden fear. 'You haven't been there? Trev, you haven't *been* there?'

Before the boy could answer, a woman had appeared,

16

racing across from one of the cul-de-sacs which bordered the allotment. She snatched the boy by the hand, gave the girl a shove which sent her reeling.

'Get away! Get away!' Her voice was shrill, even more agitated than the girl's. The look she gave Fran was one of loathing. Loathing and ... terror. 'If I had a gun,' she hissed, 'I'd shoot you!'

It wasn't until the woman and children were out of sight that Fran realised: the woman had thought she had come from over there ...

3

Sajjad Khan was alive – just. It had been two o'clock in the morning before Shahid had finally fallen asleep, slumped on the sofa in front of the television, in the middle of an old John Wayne movie. It had been almost half-past ten before he had woken again. The television had stopped working, some time during the night; not a flicker could he get out of it. Anguished, he spent the next thirty minutes trying to locate the source of the problem, frantically switching from one channel to the next, changing the fuses in the plug, testing the lights to see if it were the electricity supply. It wasn't. Panic overcame him. He couldn't stay in this place without the television! It was his sole companion, the one thing that had kept him sane. Plugged in all day to the old movies he could make believe there was still a world out there: that he was still part of it. If he didn't get his regular daily fix –

The telephone rang. He leapt at it like a wild thing, clawing up the receiver, almost slobbering in his eagerness to speak.

'Shahid?' It was his brother, Rahim. 'What happened? I didn't hear from you.'

'I only just woke up.'

'So – '

'The television's gone, I can't get anything out of it. I don't know whether it's the set or whether they've stopped transmitting. Are you getting anything out of yours?'

'I really haven't the faintest idea! It may surprise you to learn that I don't have time to sit and watch the television right now.'

'Well, could you ask Najma?' Najma was Rahim's wife.

18

She watched television all day long. She said that as her husband wouldn't let her go out and take classes, it was the only way she had of learning the language. 'Could you ask her, please? Because if yours isn't working, that would mean – '

'Have you taken leave of your senses? Talking of television at a time like this? What do I care if the thing's not working?'

Rahim didn't realise. He didn't understand. 'If one can't keep in touch – '.

'Keeping in touch was what you were supposed to do and didn't! How is my father?'

'Uh – ' The question very nearly threw him. So absorbed had he been in his frenzied attempts to restore his lifeline, he had completely forgotten the old man. He didn't dare say so to Rahim. Rahim thought Shahid should be there, dancing attendance, all the twenty-four hours of the day. It was what his mother would have done. 'Last night, I have to tell you, he was not so good.'

'And this morning?'

'This morning – uh!'

'I take it you have been in there this morning?' Rahim's voice was sharp with sudden suspicion.

'I have been in, but at this stage, you know, things can happen which – '

'Which require you to be there!'

'Wait,' said Shahid. 'I will go again and check.'

Carefully he laid the receiver by the telephone, keeping it out of range of the steady trickle of water from the flat above. Last week the trickle had been merely a damp patch on the ceiling. Even yesterday it had been no more than the occasional drip. Overnight the drip had turned to a trickle, which very soon would cascade into a flood. It was only a matter of time before the ceiling came down. But by then Shahid would be gone. He was only waiting for the old man.

The stench in the hall was definitely growing worse. Maybe it wasn't only the hall. Maybe it was the cumulative stench of all the rest of the flats. At the beginning, from his

19

vantage point on the eighth floor, he had seen furtive figures emerge, late in the evening, staggering under the weight of their shrouded loads. But that had been at the beginning; it hadn't lasted long.

He opened the door to the old man's room.

'Father?' he said. (Are you dead yet, Father?)

The thing on the bed lay still. From it came a faint but persistent high-pitched moan, like the metallic whining of an electric drill. Shahid shut the door. He went back to the sitting room, picked up the telephone.

'He is still alive.'

'Is he in pain?'

'How do I know? I can't ask him.'

'Is he still managing to eat?'

Eat? Where had Rahim been these past few weeks? Locked up in Barnet, that was where he had been. Locked up in his food emporium in a state of siege. If he had seen anyone die of this thing, he would never have asked such a question. How could you eat when –

'Shahid?'

'I'm still here.'

'Do you listen when I talk to you?'

'I listen.'

'So answer me! Is he eating?'

'He hasn't eaten for over a week.' How could you eat when your inside was all rotted away?

'Hasn't eaten anything?'

There was a silence. He knew Rahim hadn't understood. So far, in Barnet, they had been lucky.

'What have you tried him with?'

What did he expect him to try him with? A plate of vindaloo? He hadn't asked these questions when it had been the others. Rahim had always been his father's favourite. The number one son, the good boy.

'Shahid!'

'Yes.' Shahid said it sullenly. 'I haven't tried him with anything. What would be the point? He's dying.' What food there was was needed by the living. And anyway, he had seen with his mother what happened when you made them eat.

'So what are you doing for him?'

'I'm staying with him,' said Shahid. Wasn't that enough? Wasn't it *more* than enough? 'Could you ask Najma, now, please, about the television? I really need to know.'

'I'm not asking Najma about any television! You should be ashamed of yourself, worrying about so unimportant a thing as television while our father lies dying. Have you no proper feelings at all?'

He may have had, once; but they had long since gone. 'Rahim, please,' he said. 'You don't understand!'

'I understand very well! Just like always, you want to shirk your duty. Well, this time you can't! You turn your back on your own father and the curse of Allah will be on you!'

Shahid pulled a face. Stiffly he said: 'You don't have to worry, I shall stay here until it's over. But I think it's going to be over very quickly.'

'So when it is, you come to us.'

If I'm still alive, thought Shahid. He replaced the receiver and went back to the old man's room. The sound of his moaning could be heard, quite clearly, through the closed door. Shahid gritted his teeth as he turned the handle.

Why couldn't he just *die*? Didn't he realise there was nothing anyone could do for him? The others hadn't hung on and on. There were moments when he felt the old man was doing it out of sheer spite.

'What can I get you?' He forced himself to walk over and stand by the bed. 'You want water?' The jug which he had filled yesterday was still there, untouched. The water was stale and tepid. 'I'll get you some fresh.'

Fresh! That was a laugh. Since when had tap water ever qualified as fresh? Even before the epidemic ('the epidemic in the London area' was what they were calling it, all nice and self-contained) so-called drinking water had been fit only for washing motorcars. That was what Simon had

21

maintained, according to what he had read in this environmental studies book.

'It's all full of carcinogens and aluminium. Aluminium gives you Alzheimer's. So if you don't get nobbled by the Big C, you can look forward to going senile at thirty.'

Simon had talked of starting a campaign for water filters to be fitted in schools throughout the borough. In the meantime, he had said, he was going to drink nothing but bottled spa water. Poor old Si! He needn't have bothered.

Shahid refilled the jug, slid his hands into the limp balloons that had once been rubber gloves and trod back along the path to Calvary. He liked the word Calvary: he liked the concept. He knew about it because they had done it in comparative religions at school. Sajjad Khan hadn't approved, needless to say. Just as some of the white parents (though not Simon's) had complained that Christianity was being elbowed aside to make way for alien faiths, so Sajjad Khan had complained that his children were being indoctrinated with the ways of the decadent West. He had blamed the school for every hint of rebelliousness that Shahid had ever shown.

'Here! Here is your water.'

Shahid slid an arm round his father's shoulders, raising him from the pillow. A month ago, he would not have been able to do it, or not so easily. Sajjad Khan had been a big man – tall, strong, handsome. Once when Shahid had been serving in the Taj (a task he had got out of, whenever possible) he had overheard two of the customers discussing him.

'Quite a big chap, for an Indian . . . they're pretty stunted, as a rule.'

'Wouldn't be so bad-looking if he could only wipe the scowl from his face.'

Shahid had felt like dumping a load of chicken kurma over their heads. He had wanted to shout, 'He's not Indian, you fools! He's Bangladeshi!' Unfortunately, it was a fact that the restaurant had an Indian name – the Taj Mahal. It was also a fact that his father scowled. Shahid had tried telling him, once, 'It puts the customers off when you walk round like a thundercloud,' but his father had just scowled even more and told him to get on with the job and watch his tongue. He would never take advice from anyone. He had quarrelled with both his business partners, Dr Khalik and Mohsin Khan. He had quarrelled with the tandoori chef, he had quarrelled with the waiters. During school holidays, he hauled in Shahid. Shahid loathed it. He loathed having to be subservient, he loathed having to clear away the disgusting half-eaten dishes of food, the ashtrays full of cigarette butts. What he loathed most of all was the way the customers patronised.

'And how long have you been over here?'

'Do you like it in England?'

'You speak very good English!'

It would be surprising if he didn't, considering he'd been born here. His father didn't like him telling people that. He preferred him to say that he had been born in Bangladesh. He always grew angry if he heard Shahid being what he called 'too Westernised'. It wasn't what the customers wanted. They wanted atmosphere: good Muslim waiters who went to the mosque and fasted during Ramaddan and didn't smoke or drink (Sajjad Khan didn't drink but he smoked like a chimney). They didn't want an ordinary British schoolboy who was taking his A-levels and spoke English like a native.

'Just don't be so knowing all the time, the customers don't like it.'

So what if they didn't? He didn't like the customers – especially the ones that came in late, after a few drinks at the pub. They were the worst. Loud and hectoring, treating you like dirt.

'I said two pints of lager and a plate of poppadams ... let's have some service round here!'

And then let's get drunk and throw things at each other and stub our cigarette ends in the chutney and insult the waiters.

'Hey! Ali Baba! Come here, I want you!'

23

Sometimes Shahid thought that people like Rahim and his father deserved to be insulted. Once, he remembered, when Rahim had been working there (before moving to Barnet and going into business with his father-in-law), a party of Frenchmen had come in. Shahid would have liked to try out his French on them, but they had looked like the sort who might spend money so Rahim had taken over. The Frenchmen had been celebrating something: they had asked for champagne.

'What champagne do you have?'

'Oh, very good champagne, excellent champagne!' Rahim had pointed it out on the wine list. 'Bollinger champagne!' And then, seeking to impress: 'English, of course.'

Shahid had thought the Frenchmen were going to have apoplexies on the spot. Two of them had just sat and stared, the third, in tones of disbelief, had said, 'English champagne?' Some people at a table nearby had started laughing. Rahim, the fool, thinking they were laughing at the Frenchmen, had turned and whispered, 'Foreigners!' which had made them laugh even more. Shahid could have climbed into the wallpaper.

They had all been an embarrassment to him; all his family. Twenty years on the assembly line at Ford's (as Sajjad Khan had been proud of telling people), and still his father couldn't speak the language properly. There had been an excuse for his grandmother; for his mother, too. Like Najma, she had a husband who believed in keeping her in her place. (Unlike Najma, she came from a generation which believed in women being kept there.) There was no excuse for Rahim, and not very much more for Fatima. Shahid had tried, with Fatima.

'You're living in England, you must learn to be English!'

All she had said was, 'Why? When I am not?'

'Because if you don't,' Shahid had said, 'you will never fit in.'

Fatima had just tossed her head and said she didn't want to fit in. It had embarrassed him terribly while she was still at school, everyone knowing that she was his sister. Everyone thinking that just because *she* wouldn't go to parties or discos or mix with members of the opposite sex, then neither would he. It had been bitter for Shahid, wanting more than anything to be accepted.

Roshana was the only one who hadn't shamed him. He had been proud of Roshana. Six years old and already using a vocabulary larger than Rahim's and his father's put together. She wouldn't have grown up to be bullied and humiliated. She would have been like him, liberal, twentieth-century, independent. He and Rosh –

He stopped. It was dangerous, thinking of Roshana. It was all right to think of the others; but not of her. If he thought of her – no, well, he wouldn't. He would think of other things. He would think of –

Nursery rhymes.

Hickory dickory *dock*

The mouse ran up the *clock*

The clock struck one

The mouse ran down

Hickory dickory –

With a grunt, Sajjad Khan's head suddenly slumped forward on to his chest, almost knocking the glass of water from Shahid's hand. From out of his mouth, without any warning, came a jet of black vomit, thick and stinking.

'Eeyurgh!' A convulsive shudder ran through Shahid. With a scream, he sprang to his feet. The water went over the floor: Sajjad Khan, unsupported, fell sideways across the bed. Shahid bolted.

Out in the kitchen, feverish and panic-stricken, he wrenched both taps as full as they would go, thrust both hands beneath the gushing water, watched as the black gunge swirled away down the drain. Water splatted everywhere, cascading up the walls, flobbing in great puddles to the floor, until Shahid and the whole kitchen were saturated. Still, obsessively, he went on sluicing. He sluiced until he had counted to ten thousand without any cheating. Only then, still wearing the gloves, did he strip off his wet clothes, cramming them in the cupboard beneath the sink, out of sight, slamming the door on them, before carefully unscrewing the cap on his last precious bottle of bleach, shaking his hands free of the gloves and starting on a minute inspection, back, front, fingers splayed, for any signs of broken skin.

There was a small pinprick on the inside first joint of the little finger of his right hand. So small it could just barely be seen. Could have been a splinter, perhaps, or a tiny nick. He worried at it, squinting at it, over by the window, bending the tip of his finger back to try and see whether the skin was actually punctured. He thought that it was. His blood froze. He felt the goose bumps break out all up and down his spine. Naked, he streaked back across the kitchen, through the sloshing water, to plunge his hand into a bowl full of neat bleach.

He didn't *think* any of the sludge had seeped through into the glove; but he wasn't taking any chances.

Everyone had to have a mask; the child had said so.

The child had also said that you could get through the closed-up house in The Mount by way of the cellar. He had been right about that. The cellar windows had been boarded up, but someone had wrenched one of the boards away, making a hole just big enough for a person not too fat to squeeze through. It had been scary, down in the cellar: dank and musty, full of menace. Shapes had loomed, unidentifiable in the grey dark. She had barked her shin on something hard, stubbed her toe into something soft. The something hard had hurt, but the something soft had frightened her. Only the faint hint of daylight, coming through the hole in the boarded-up window, had given her the courage to carry on: only the desperate need to get home had given her the courage to go down there in the first place.

Now she stood in the sunlight, on the other side of the houses. Everything looked so normal! So ordinary and Sundayish. But still everyone had to have a mask. The child had said so.

26

Frantically, Fran set her rucksack on the ground and crouched beside it, delving amongst the contents. She had nothing that would serve as a mask! No scarf, no handkerchief; only paper tissues. A voice inside her said, 'You've got a sweat-shirt! Use that.'

Slowly, foolishly, clasping the sweat-shirt, Fran stood up. Even now she hesitated.

She remembered once, on a school trip to London, with Harry when they were seniors, they had all crammed on to a crowded tube train at Oxford Circus, and Fran, straphanging, separated from the rest, had spotted a brown paper parcel down on the floor amongst people's legs. She had been sure it was a bomb, about to go off. When they had left the train, a few stops later, the brown paper bag had still been there. She had told Harry about it afterwards, thinking Harry would laugh. Instead, Harry had screeched, 'Fran, that's *awful*! Why didn't you say anything? People could have been killed!'

Harry would have said something. She wouldn't have cared that the brown paper parcel might turn out to be only somebody's sandwiches or dirty washing. Harry had more sense.

What would Harry say now?

'For Heaven's sake, Fran! Do you want to *die*?'

Fumbling, with hands made clumsy by the sudden pit of terror opening up within her, Fran smothered her face in the sweat-shirt, yanked the sleeves into a knot at the back of her head, swung her rucksack over one shoulder and ran.

Raglan Court opened directly off The Mount; an ordinary, undistinguished, south suburban street. Fran had lived there all her life. She knew every garden, every house. The house on the corner, with its monkey puzzle tree: the house called Mardi, which had pretensions to grandeur (wrought-iron railings and brass coach lamps). Number fifteen, with its wonderful green shutters with the heart-shaped spy holes, which had so intrigued Fran as a child: number twenty-three, where the poor mad lady in the bobble hat sat and waved at people through the window. Fran always

27

made a point of smiling and waving back. She didn't today because the mad lady wasn't there.

Nobody was there. The road was empty. Nobody gardened, nobody car-washed. There were no children playing on the little green at the end. But it was the absence of sound which struck her almost more than the absence of people; people, after all, could be indoors. But no radio, no television, no traffic –

'Mum! Oh, Mum!'

Fran threw open the front gate, half fell up the path, flung herself at the front door.

'Mum!' she cried. 'Mum, let me in!'

4

'*Mum!*' There was no reply to her frantic knocking. 'Mum, it's me . . . it's Fran!'

Fran poked open the flap of the letter-box and peered through. The house seemed deserted. But the hallway, with its chocolate brown carpet, looked reassuringly just the same as always. She could make out the usual vase of fresh-cut flowers on the chest at the far end, her dad's walking stick – his knobkerrie, as he called it – standing in its appointed place by the hall table.

Maybe . . . maybe they were just in the back garden and hadn't heard her knocking.

Fran unlatched the side gate and ran down the narrow passage which divided number ten from the house next door.

'Mum?' The back garden was empty. (She noticed, without really taking it in, that her father's beloved flower-beds looked parched and uncared for.)

'*Mum!*' Fran hurled herself at the kitchen door, rattling the handle, but it was locked. There was a spare key hidden beneath one of the stones in the rockery. She sprang across the lawn, across grass that was yellow and straw-like – her dad's *lawn* – scrabbled for the key in its polythene wrapping, raced back with it to the house. Her hand was shaking so that she could scarcely fit the key into the lock. (It had always been a bit wonky. 'We must do something about that lock,' her mum used to say; but her dad had been too busy, tending to his garden.)

The kitchen looked just as it always looked: neat, clean, scrubbed. Everything in its place: the mugs in a row on their hooks; saucepans in the rack; tea, coffee, sugar, salt,

29

all lined up just where they ought to be. There was only one thing which wasn't where it ought to be, and that was a jar of marmalade, standing on the formica-topped table. It was being used as a paperweight, securing some sheets of writing paper. Fran raced across the kitchen and snatched them up.

Dearest darling Fran –

It was her mum's writing.

I don't know if you will ever come back to read this, but I am writing it for you just in case. I would hate to go without saying goodbye to you.

Go? Go where? Fran's heart thudded painfully against her ribs. She felt suddenly very cold.

Your dad died yesterday. He was ill for four days, he suffered so, I was glad when it was over for him. It will not be long for me. There is nothing anyone can do for us, we're all on our own now. Nobody wants to know anyone else. You can't really blame them, there are people with young families to consider. They are the ones I feel for. For myself I don't mind, it's you young ones I worry about. I wouldn't want to go on living without your dad, he meant all the world to me, but you've still got so much ahead of you. All your tomorrows still to come. Please God it will burn itself out and everything will go back to normal.

They're calling it the London plague, I don't know if that is because it is only in London or because it started in London. There isn't any way of finding out. I have tried several times to ring your gran but something has happened to the telephones, it seems you can only speak to people in the London area. Your dad says the Government have done it on purpose to stop panic. He could be right, I suppose they have to do these things in time of emergency. But I am praying that where you are you will be spared.

Nobody seems to know what is the cause of it all. Some people say it's terrorists, that they've put something in the water, but I think it is just one of those things. We've been so wicked, destroying the beauty of the world, maybe this is our punishment.

I don't think they would let you come back while the epidemic is still on, but everything is so turned upside down and we have so little news of the outside that nobody can really know what is happening. But if you do come back before they have set things to rights and tidied up, I will tell you, so you will know, that we will both be upstairs. But Fran, my darling, I would rather you didn't come and look for us, it is not a nice sight. I want you to remember us how we were, when we were all a happy family together. Do you remember those wonderful holidays we had, down in Cornwall with your gran? We had such lovely times. I would like to think things will all go back to being what they used to be, and you will grow up and get married and have a family of your own. Then you can talk to them about the old days and how happy we were.

Tell your gran I tried to telephone her. I have tried lots of times but I cannot get through.

Darling, I shall be long gone by the time you read this, if you ever do read it. Remember the good times and try not to be too sad. I know it will not be easy, but your dad and I care so much for you. We want only for you to be happy. So don't grieve too much, just get on with living your life. For our sake.

Goodbye, darling.

All my dearest love,
Mum.

Fran sat, with the tears coursing down her cheeks, soaking into the sweat-shirt which she still had tied round her nose and mouth. She looked at the date on the letter: Wednesday, 11 August. Over a fortnight ago. What had Fran been doing, a fortnight ago? Collecting firewood, preparing meals, counting the days until she could come home . . . Fran, not knowing, and Mum sitting here –

Mum! Oh, Mum!

Fran blotted at her eyes with the edge of her sweat-shirt. She stood up. Listened. Not a sound. Slowly she moved across to the door. Opened it; just a crack. Listened again. Eased the door wider, little bit by little bit, listening, listening, keeping herself shielded, behind the door, in case of – what? She hardly liked to think.

Out in the hall, on the table against which rested her father's knobkerrie, were two foil envelopes, one sealed, one which had been opened. Fran paused, to look. SURGIMASK© it said, in big red letters against the silver foil. And then, in smaller letters underneath, A Trademark of British Surgical Industries.

Numbly, Fran tore open the sealed packet and pulled out the contents. A surgical mask, just as the two children and the woman had been wearing. She put it on, untying the arms of her sweat-shirt and letting it fall to the floor; and then, because it wasn't fair to make a mess, just because Mum wasn't here any more to tidy things away after her, she bent and picked it up again. It was still Mum's home. Mum would be hurt if she could see Fran just dropping things and leaving them.

She folded the sweat-shirt neatly, and placed it on the table. She noticed as she did so that the flowers in the vase at the end of the hall were dead. There was no post lying on the mat, there had been no milk outside the door. Did that mean they weren't delivering milk and post any more? Or did it – could it –

'Mum!' called Fran. 'Mum, are you there?'

Suddenly, urgently, she was galloping up the stairs, three at a time, just like she always used to. ('Fran! You'll bring the house down!')

'Mum?'

Mum and Dad were in the bedroom. She knew they were Mum and Dad because – because they couldn't be anyone else, and because – well, because they were wearing Mum and Dad's clothes. Dad's red pyjamas and Mum's nylon nightie, the one they had laughed at, with all the frills, which Fran had made her buy.

'I couldn't wear that! I'd look like a middle-aged tart.'

'No, you wouldn't. Go on! Buy it.'

Had Mum put it on specially, for dying in? 'Go on, Fran, have a good laugh! Silly old woman, dolling herself up – '

God! Oh, God! Fran lurched fron the room, hand pressed to the mask which covered her mouth. At the foot of the stairs she fell in a heap, her head on the floor, her fists beating. A convulsive knot of anguish tightened inside her. Terrible and disgusting noises – long shuddering rasps followed by a deep baying like the howl of a wounded beast – echoed round the hall. Fran hardly connected them with herself. She heard a voice wailing –

'Muu-u-u-um! Mu-u-u-u-um! I want my mu-u-u-um!'

The wailing faded, moderated to a muted whimper. The raspings and the bayings gave way to weeping. Steadily, inexorably, like a downpour of rain, the tears came washing over her. Fran raised her head. She pulled out her handkerchief and blew her nose beneath the mask; then awkwardly, still whimpering, lumbered via hands and knees like an old person to her feet.

Mum had a front door key in her bag, but Mum's bag was sacrosanct. And anyway, it was in the bedroom. Fran stumbled over to the door, opened it, set it on the latch and took the short cut across the front garden, over the low hedge, to Mrs Evans at number twelve.

There was no answer at number twelve; nor number eight. At number six she thought she saw a curtain twitch, but still nobody came. At number five, across the road, she saw a face looking at her from an upstairs window. She was sure of it, this time; it was definitely a face. She didn't know the people who lived at number five, but Mum would have done. Mum knew everyone.

Fran ran across and up the path and rang and rang at the front door, and banged with the knocker, and called through the letter-box, 'It's Fran Latimer from number ten!' but whoever the owner of the face had been they weren't coming down to talk to her.

In panic she ran back across the road.

'Help me! Somebody please help me!'

But there wasn't anyone; or if there was they were certainly not coming out to help a crazy person, lolloping in the gutters and shrieking.

Harry, she thought. She would ring Harry!

Fran changed direction and bolted back up the road. The front door on its latch was sent flying against the wall, then slammed shut with such force it instantly flew open again. A shaft of sunlight filtered through, warm and golden in the darkness, before slowly the door fell back, banged, and this time stayed shut.

Fran clawed at the telephone, dialling Harry's number with a finger so unsteady it kept skidding out of the dialling hole so that in the end she had to pick up the telephone pencil on its length of plastic coil and use that.

The telephone rang, and went on ringing. Fran rocked, kneeling on the floor. To and fro, to and fro ... God! oh, God! oh, God!

The ringing stopped. Someone at the other end had picked up the receiver. There was a silence. Fran said, 'Harry?' in a voice as small and tremulous as a child's.

Still the silence went on.

'Hallo?' said Fran. Her voice quavered. 'Harry? Auntie Ellen? Is there anybody there?'

There was a sound, like a swift intake of breath, then a voice said, 'Fran?'

'*Harry!*' She could have sobbed for sheer relief. 'Oh, Harry . . .'

'You're back! I wasn't expecting you for hours! Did you have a good time? Have you lost any weight? I have! I've been on a diet, my waist is down to *eighteen* . . . honestly! I can get into the Victorian dress. I'll show you, I'll put it on for you – '

Harry's voice babbled forth, bright and incongruous, into the telephone. Fran sat there, stunned.

'Are you coming round? We've got some new stuff in the shop, it's fabulous. There's something here that would really suit you, specially if you've gone all nice and thin. It doesn't suit me, but it would look smashing on you. You're the right height for it. When are you going to come? How long have you been back? Have you had your lunch yet?'

Fran just managed to say, 'Harry – ' before her voice broke and the tears engulfed her. How could Harry not know? Not be aware? Even if she didn't know about – about Mum and Dad –

'*Have* you?'

Fran made a negative mumbling noise into the receiver. Something was wrong. Harry *couldn't* not be aware. Mum's letter –

'Don't bother about lunch! Come over anyway.' A sudden urgency had entered Harry's voice. 'Fran, come now!'

Fran wiped the back of her hand across her eyes. 'All right. I'm coming.'

'Don't stop to do anything. Just *come*.'

The dress shop called Janetta, owned by Harry's mum, was in the High Street, only a few minutes' away. Harry and Mrs Somers lived in a small flat above. There were only the two of them; Harry's dad had disappeared many years ago, before Harry had even started at kindergarten.

The High Street was deserted; in all the long road there was not another living creature to be seen. Not a dog, not a cat, not even the odd drunk in the gutter. A few cars were parked, but all were empty. Fran no longer thought how pleasant not to have diesel fumes and the noise of traffic. She would have given anything for diesel fumes now.

Janetta's, when she reached it, looked just the same as always. The only thing which struck her was that the window display had not been changed; it was still the deep roses and purples that it had been in July. Harry's mum was good at window displays, she changed them regularly, a different colour for each month. August was going to have

35

been yellow – all the shades from palest primrose through to deepest ochre. She and Fran had discussed it.

'Yellow's such a nice, bright, *summery* colour.'

Fran reached out her hand to press the bell for the flat. As she did so she became aware of something flitting, floating, fluttering on the edge of her field of vision. She turned her head, and saw that it was Harry. Harry, in the shop window, dressed as if for a party in the Victorian dress, all red tartan with its pinched-in waist and crinolined skirt and foamy white petticoat sticking out underneath like a frill.

'Harry?' Fran moved across to the shop door. Harry opened it, just a sliver – 'Get in, get in!' – then closed and bolted it and went dancing away across the floor in the sunlight, laughing, twirling, making the crinoline hoop and spin.

'Look! I told you I could wear it!'

Fran swallowed. The Victorian dress had been bought by Mrs Somers at a theatrical costumiers, years ago, for a special Christmas window display; it was child-sized. The last time Harry had been able to get into it was when she was thirteen. (Fran not since she was eleven.)

'Harry – ' Fran stopped. 'You're not wearing a mask!'

By way of reply, still laughing, Harry whipped a chiffon scarf from her waist, where she had tied it, and wound it over the lower part of her face. Then, coquettishly, bobbing and bouncing, showing off to Fran, she weaved her way about the shop, roguishly peeping through a rail full of dresses, coyly posing before a mirror, snatching a straw hat from a stand and cramming it down over her curls.

Fran stood watching, helpless and bewildered. This wasn't Harry! It was like a caricature of Harry. She was never this silly, this frivolous, this – this *infantile*.

'I told you, didn't I?' Harry gave another little spin, kicking a leg up behind her as she did so. 'You're not the only one who can lose weight!'

Harry hadn't needed to lose weight, she had been quite

thin enough to begin with. 'Elfin', Fran's mum had called her.

'Harry,' cried Fran, 'what have you been doing?'

'Slimming!' Harry gurgled, merrily, and made her eyes go big. They looked like deep pits of coal in her pinched face. 'Come and see what I've got for you! It's one of the new autumn dresses, we haven't unpacked them properly yet, come and see!' She took Fran's hand, trying to coax her across to the storeroom. Fran resisted.

'What's the matter?' Harry pouted. 'Oh, I haven't asked you how the camp went! Well, how *did* it go? Who was there? What were they like? What did you eat? What did you do? Did you enjoy it? Well, come on, tell me! Don't just stand there! Tell tell tell!'

Fran bit her lip behind her mask. Harry didn't appear to think it odd that Fran should be wearing a mask. Nor had she questioned Fran's assertion that she, too, should be wearing one. That meant . . . that could only mean she did know, but – but that she –

'Tell me, tell me, tell!' Harry was dancing up and down, clapping her hands like a little girl. 'Tell me, tell me, t – '

'The camp was great.'

'I knew it would be! I knew you'd like it! I s – '

'Harry, why is the road out there so quiet?'

'Is it? I hadn't noticed. Because it's Sunday, I suppose.' Harry's tone was offhand. 'If you're not going to tell me any more let's go and try on the new stock.'

'What about your mum?'

'Mum won't mind.'

'Harry, where is your mum?'

'Oh! I don't know. Upstairs somewhere. In her room.' Harry swooshed with both hands at her crinoline, making it rock upwards showing all her petticoat. She giggled. 'These things are *fun!*'

'Can we go and see her?'

'Afterwards; later. When we've tried dresses on.'

'Harry, I want to see her now!'

'What for?'

'Please, Harry!'

'Oh, you're such a *spoilsport*.' Harry stamped a foot, pouting as she used to at juniors. *Harriet Somers, you are a very impudent little girl* . . . 'I want to try things on!'

Gently Fran said, 'We can do that later. When we've seen your mum. Come on!' She held out a hand. Harry took it obediently, though still with her lower lip stuck out as a sign of displeasure.

Together they climbed the stairs to the flat. Fran noticed, as they neared the top, that Harry's hand in hers had begun to tremble.

'Where is she?' said Fran. 'In her bedroom?'

Harry's finger went to her mouth. Like a child, she nibbled and tore at a piece of skin. 'I'm not to go in there.'

'It's all right,' said Fran. 'I'll go.'

Watched by a big-eyed Harry, she knocked at the bedroom door. Twice she knocked but there was no reply; she supposed, in her heart, she hadn't really expected one. She looked across at Harry, shrunk against the wall at the top of the stairs. Harry was still watching her. She knew she had to go in.

Bracing herself, she turned the handle. It had been like this at school once, she remembered. A time in juniors when Harry had thought it amusing to stretch a length of nylon twine across the corridor at ankle level, then hide and watch the fun. Poor old Fossil had come doddering along in her bi-focals, with her nose in a book as usual, and taken a terrible dive. She had gone down and not got up again. It had been Fran who had had to go and investigate, not Harry. Yet it had always been Harry who had the ideas, Fran who meekly followed.

'Auntie Ellen?' She whispered it apologetically, just in case. 'It's me, Fran.'

There was no need to have whispered; she knew it as soon as she opened the door. Perhaps even as she was turning the handle. There was a something, a terrible, gut-churning, deep-inside sort of something, which already she was beginning to recognise. She hadn't noticed it at home until

38

she had come to Harry's and found it here as well. She knew it now for what it was. But oh, Harry's mum! Harry's beautiful, elegant mum! Oh, Harry, she thought, how could you? How could you let her lie there like that? If I had been at home, thought Fran, I would not have let it happen to Mum and Dad. She would have tended them so lovingly. They would not have been left to sink in a mire of squalor and stench. Harry, oh, Harry! How could you?

Harry was no longer at the top of the stairs. Fran found her down in the storeroom, holding up dresses and looking at herself in one of the full-length mirrors.

'Harry,' she said, 'your mum – '

'Is she dead? Most people are. I expect we shall be soon. Do you like this green one? Look, it has a zip all the way down the back. Do you want to try it? I think there's one your size. It would suit you. Now that you're back we could have a dress parade. We could try on every single thing – '

'Didn't you even call the doctor?' said Fran.

'Hello, doctor, my mummy's dying. Ho ho ho, little girl, and what do you want me to do? Come round and give you a potion? Oh, they're very cunning, these doctors! You have to watch them.'

'You mean, you didn't do anything?'

'What did you want me to do?' Harry whirled, flirtatiously, holding the green dress before her. '*Anything you can do, I can do better, I can do anything better than you!*' She carolled it happily as she sorted through the assembled rack of dresses, looking for one that would fit Fran. The one she had originally picked out had been left in a crumpled heap on the floor, along with several others. '*I say potato and you say potahto, I say tomayto and you say t* – here we are! Size twelve. You must be a size twelve by now. All that healthy living. Did you eat nuts and lentils and split-pea cutlets? My wrist is better, by the way. Had you noticed?' She drooped her hand, to show. 'No plaster. I got sick of it so I hacked it off with the bread knife. It was ever so difficult, you wouldn't believe! First I had to bash it with a ham – '

39

Harry broke off. Her eyes had gone big again, her face drawn and white.

'It's only the telephone,' said Fran. She suddenly realised the significance of what she had said. *Telephone*. She turned and raced from the storeroom, full pelt into the shop.

'Don't answer it!' Harry was hot on her heels. She flew at Fran, almost knocking the receiver out of her hands. 'Don't answer it!'

'Harry, don't be *stupid*.' Fran fended her off with one hand, keeping the earpiece pressed close. 'Hallo?'

A male voice, educated, pleasant-sounding, said: 'Hallo! And how are you today?'

'Oh, you must want Harry.' It was obviously a family friend. Maybe a neighbour. 'Just a minute, I'll – '

'No, don't go away! I don't want Harry. You'll do very nicely. You sound like a nice young girl. I like young girls. Shall I tell you what I like to do with them? First of all I – '

Fran's cheeks flared. She slammed the receiver down.

'I told you not to answer it,' said Harry. 'He does it every day. I thought it was him earlier, when it was you. I knew it'd be him this time. He's the only one left that ever rings. Sometimes I think he's the only person left that's still alive. I hate him! I hate him!' Harry's voice rose to a scream. She was twisting and tearing at the dress she had picked out for Fran. 'I wish he'd drop dead!'

The small kitchen at the back of the flat looked like a refuse tip. The cupboards, when Fran had managed to wade through the sea of empty tins and crushed milk cartons which littered the floor, turned out to be bare. She found just one packet of drinking chocolate and half a bag of rice. In the fridge there was nothing at all. When she asked Harry how long it was since she had had a proper meal, Harry just pouted and said, 'Don't need proper meals . . . I'm *slimming*.'

Living so near to the shops, Harry's mum had never bothered building food mountains. She had been in the habit of just popping over the road or going down the market

40

when she wanted anything. Fran thought that it must have been some time since just popping over the road had been possible. She tried asking Harry if any of the shops were still open, but even though Harry didn't reply – she had gone waltzing off in the Victorian dress to put the television on – Fran knew what the answer must be. She hadn't seen a single shop that was open in all the long walk from Purley.

At home there would be food. Mum had always kept the cupboards well stocked. Dad had teased her sometimes; accused her of having a siege mentality. (Did you thank her for it, Dad, when there really was a siege? Or weren't you in a state to appreciate it?) She hoped Mum had had just a little moment of gratification, looking at all her tins and packets, before the nightmare closed in.

'Are you coming to watch the telly?' Harry had danced back again; light as air with her eighteen-inch waist. 'There's a film on . . . *Seven Brides for Seven Brothers*. Old musical. Just your sort of thing. Are you coming?'

'I'm hungry,' said Fran. 'I've got to eat something.'

'Oh!' Harry pulled an impatient face. Fran and her common sense . . . But you couldn't not eat; not unless –

Firmly, Fran pushed the thought to the back of her mind. Mum wouldn't like her to do that. Mum wanted her to survive; to get married and have a family so that she could tell them about the old times. Because wherever she was, Mum would know what was going on. She would be terribly distressed if Fran just gave up. Mum had been through enough without that. Fran owed it to her to make an effort.

'*Fran!*' Harry tugged at her.

'Harry, we have to eat.' If they went back to the house there wouldn't only be food but they would be safe from intruders. And the obscene telephone caller couldn't get at them there bcause he wouldn't know the number. 'If we went back to my place – '

'Went back to your place?' Harry's eyes grew wide and fearful. 'Went *out*?'

Why not? thought Fran. It was still light, there was no

41

one out there. And yet, like Harry, she found she didn't want to.

'Eat that!' Harry pointed to the rice and the drinking chocolate. 'That'll do if you're hungry.'

She let herself be persuaded. Tomorrow she would go back.

They spent the evening sitting on the sofa watching old films on television. It seemed terrible at first, to be watching television in the same flat where Harry's mother lay untended; but as Harry said, when Fran nervously suggested that perhaps they should be doing something else, 'What else is there to do?' Fran didn't like to say, 'We ought to bury your mum's body.' And in any case how could they do it? The yard outside was concrete. Instead she said, 'We could tidy the flat – get rid of the rubbish.'

'What for?' said Harry. 'Oh, look, there's Omar!' *Seven Brides for Seven Brothers* had come to an end: they were watching *Dr Zhivago* now. Omar Sharif in a fur hat striding through the snow.

'Isn't there any news?' said Fran.

'What d'you want news for?'

'Harry, I've been away for a month! I don't know what's been going on!'

'Nothing's been going on. It's all been just as boring as it always is. Stop nagging at me! I want to watch Omar.'

The only news that there was came right at the end of the film, when a solemn-faced newsreader, whom Fran had never seen before, appeared on the screen and announced that 'the epidemic in the London area is still being contained. Travelling restrictions remain in force but it is hoped that normal communication links with the capital and surrounding zone will be restored shortly. In the meantime, the Government has just announced that as from midday today ten of the largest cities in the UK were placed under the same restrictions as Greater London. These cities are Birmingham, Liverpool, Manchester – '

The list went on. Fran turned, white-faced, to look at

42

Harry, but Harry, already, was on her knees by the television, pressing the buttons in search of more entertainment.

'They've had some really good films lately . . . all the old ones. I mean, really old ones. They had Marilyn Monroe the other night. She was quite prettyish, I suppose, but my goodness was she *fat*! She certainly didn't have an eighteen-inch waist. Then they had this one with Audrey Hepburn called *Breakfast at Tiffany's* – '

The pictures on the television came and went as Harry punched her way through the channels. Fran heard '. . . Government spokesman stressed these were only precautionary measures and that there was no need to panic.'

She wondered where the Government was.

5

They slept, that night, in one of the small storerooms, down in the basement, where Mrs Somers kept all the out-of-date, hard-to-sell items which she was saving for the sales. Harry had dragged her bedding from upstairs and made a nest for herself amongst the boxes, using her duvet as a mattress, a pile of coats to cover herself. It was chilly down there in the basement, yet airless, too; windowless, like a tomb, with only one small vent set high up near the ceiling. The door, originally, had had no lock on the inside, but Harry – Harry the impractical, who couldn't even knock in a nail without bending it double or hammering her thumb – had fixed heavy bolts top and bottom and a big padlock and chain. A bulb, unshaded, cast a harsh white glare, trying to the eyes, yet neither of them had suggested turning it off, nor did it occur to Fran that now there were two of them they might transfer to somewhere less spartan. After that telephone call she could understand why Harry should want to shut herself away behind a locked door in a windowless room.

In the old days when they had stayed with each other they had always lain awake talking deep into the small hours – or at least, Harry had done so. She used to complain rather bitterly that Fran had a habit of suddenly going to sleep and 'leaving me awake all by myself'. Tonight it was Harry rather than Fran who fell asleep, her old green duffel coat pulled up over her head; Fran who was left on her own, wide awake.

There was a radio by her side, the little old transistor which Harry had had for her tenth birthday. She longed to turn it on, to hear voices and music, be reassured that somewhere out there there were still people going about

44

their normal everyday business, but she didn't dare for fear of waking Harry.

She tossed and turned on the duvet. It seemed full of lumps. At last, unable to bear the discomfort any longer, she slipped her hand beneath the layers of cardboard which Harry had spread underneath. Her fingers encountered something hard and cold.

Cautiously she eased her weight off it and slid it out: it was the big kitchen carving knife with serrated edges. She looked at it for a long moment, then slowly pushed it back. If she had been by herself, she rather thought that she, too, would have slept with a carving knife.

As she restored the knife to its resting place beneath the cardboard her hand came into contact with something else. Something . . . firm and regular. It felt like a book. She pulled it out and found that it was Harry's diary.

This is the diary of me, Harriet Margaret Somers, begun in the year of my thirteenth birthday, to be continued until the day of my death whenever that shall be. In this present year of Our Lord I am sixteen years old. I have now kept this journal for three years and nine months. None shall be privy to what I write herein, none shall even be aware of its existence save for my very good friend Frances Ruth Latimer into whose care and safe keeping I commend it should anything of an untoward nature chance to befall me.

(Signed) Harriet M. Somers

Fran remembered Harry making that inscription. She had just finished reading *The Tower of London* by Harrison Ainsworth. Everything she had written for the whole of the winter term had been what Mrs Dainty called 'Heavily under the influence . . . I wish you'd chosen someone who wrote ordinary modern English! Preferably of the British rather than the American variety. But anything rather than all this pish-tushery!'

Fran sat, clasping the diary, holding it tight to resist

temptation. Would it be a betrayal, to read what Harry had written? In ordinary circumstances such an idea would never have occurred to her. Diaries were private; almost the most private possession a person could have. But these were not ordinary circumstances! Harry would forgive her: she would understand. In any case, she and Fran traditionally read bits from their diaries to each other. Not just when one of them had been away, but regularly, once a month, either in Fran's bedroom or in Harry's, they had held their reading sessions. She and Harry didn't have secrets – and besides, she needed to know!

Guiltily, in spite of her rationalisations, Fran glanced down at Harry, curled in a heap beside her. She was still fast asleep, making little whiffling noises beneath her mound of coats.

Turning on her side, Fran opened the diary.

Friday 16 July
Simon Dobson said in class today that all our drinking water has aluminium in it, which means we shall all go senile by the time we're thirty. He wants everyone to sign a petition for water filters in schools.

Fran remembered that. She remembered the incident, and she remembered Harry reading it out to her from the diary. It was the last reading session they had had before Fran had gone away. They had discussed Simon Dobson and agreed that he had double standards.

'Always lecturing people,' Harry had grumbled. 'Always going on about people being gullible and believing what they read in the papers, but whenever they have a story that knocks the Government he's quick enough to believe *that*.'

Nevertheless, they had signed the petition just in case.

Fran flipped on through the pages – quietly, furtively, uneasy in her conscience even now – until she came to the end of July.

46

Friday 30 July

Fran went off to camp today. It's going to be horrid without her. Why did I have to go and break my wrist *now*? I don't see why I couldn't have gone with it in plaster, it's just Mum and the doctor behaving like old women. Mum isn't usually like that. She says she wouldn't mind if it was an ordinary camp but the whole point of this one is for people to live rough. I don't know how Fran will manage without me, she's not at all a rough sort of person. I'm quite tough and pushy but Fran is, well, nicer I suppose. I do hope she'll be all right.

Saturday 31 July

I do miss Fran! We had some new stock in today from Pierre Rosenthal, Mum let me help sort it. She let me try on some of the dresses, they're gorgeous. There's some that would really suit Fran. I wonder if she'll manage to lose weight? NB: I AM GOING TO GO ON A DIET!!!

Sunday 1 August

Bumped into Simon Dobson in the Whitgift Centre this morning. He asked me if I'd like to go and have a coffee with him, so I did. I think he might fancy me a bit, or maybe it's just because Shahid Khan is going out with Julie Onslow (!!!) and SD's nose is out of joint. I don't mind just having a coffee but if he's going to suggest anything else, like a disco or something, I shall say no. SD is OK but basically he is still a chauvinist whatever he likes to pretend, and anyway it would be disloyal to Fran, especially when she is not here to know about it.

Monday 2 August

There is some kind of an epidemic happening in London. All the papers had headlines about it and it was on the news, every time you turned the television on there was someone saying not to panic, it is under control, etc., but no one has said what it is exactly, just that it's an epidemic. SD rang up this evening and said would I go to a disco with him next week. I said jokingly, trying to get out of it, that if this epidemic comes to Croydon we won't be around to go to any disco and he said that might be more true than I realised. He said he didn't think the newspapers were being honest about it and that things were far more serious than they were letting on, but SD is like that, he thinks everything is a Government plot. Anyway, I just made noises about the disco. We shall see.

Tuesday 3 August

SD is right for once: the epidemic *is* more serious than they said. Today we had surgical masks put through the letter-box and all the newsreaders on television are wearing them, even if they are not in London, just to show people that they have to. I didn't want to at first, it felt really stupid, going round with a mask over your face, but Mum said it would feel even more stupid to go and catch this disease, whatever it is. She said better safe than sorry. I said, that is a cliché, but Mum said things are only clichés because they are universal truths. I wish she would tell that to Mrs Dainty . . .

Wednesday 4 August

Nobody seems to know what this disease is, or if they do they're not telling. One minute they say it's a virus, the next minute they say it's terrorist groups trying to poison us. SD rang up and said the disco was off because of all places of entertainment being closed. I don't mind about not going to the disco but now you can't even go for a coffee. The Government has said that only essential service places are allowed to be open. It's because they don't want lots of people all gathered together in one place. I tried being funny and saying that it was all a Government plot but he took it seriously and said that although he didn't think it was a plot he did think the Government knew more than they were letting on. Of course he would say that, but maybe it is true and they don't want to cause panic.

Thursday 5 August

The symptoms of this disease are: headache, high temperature, sore throat, aches and pains and being sick. Like flu, only a thousand times worse. Later on you get black blotches which mean your insides are rotting. *There is no cure.* But if you wear your mask and use gloves for touching anyone that has it you will be all right. SD has a theory it is something to do with germ warfare. HE WOULD.

Friday 6 August

The Government is no longer in London! They announced it on the television today. It's an emergency measure while the epidemic is on, but they haven't said where they have gone to. In the meantime, all the rest of us are stuck here! There have been no trains running for the past week and nobody is allowed in or out. SD said what else did I expect? He is going to ring me every day until things are back to normal. He is quite nice I suppose.

Saturday 7 August

Now there is no milk being delivered!! So no cereal for breakfast. This is worse than the Stone Age! I wish Fran was here. How will she get back if they are still not letting people in or out? It's not just London itself but all the boroughs. There is a road block down by the Red Deer manned by soldiers. SD told me this when he rang. He said he'd been down to look and they will actually shoot anyone who tries to get out. According to him, we are now living in a Fascist state, but Mum says they have to contain it, it is just our bad luck that we live in the wrong part of the country. But if we keep our heads down and stay indoors we will be all right. That is the message: don't go out unless you absolutely have to.

Sunday 8 August

I am very angry! They have cancelled all the television progs without telling us – well, not all, but all my favourite ones. *Families* was not on! And nobody said why not or when it would be back. How can I live without knowing what Randy Rodge is up to? SD says he thinks that some people in his road have got the disease.

Monday 9 August

Families not on again. Just mouldy old boring films. Mum went out to the shops this morning. I was scared and didn't want her to, but she said she had to as we have almost no food left. I would rather live without food until it is safe to go out. However, I offered to go with her but she wouldn't let me. She took the car and said she wouldn't be long. She was away almost three hours and I was petrified, I thought something must have happened to her, but it was only that none of the shops are open any more, not even the supermarkets. Mum says people are just breaking in and taking what they can find. She had to drive round until she was able to find something and even then she was not able to find very much. She is worried it will not last us but I said we will ration ourselves. This epidemic surely cannot go on for very much longer, or if it does the Government will do something. Mum says it is very ghostly and creepy out there, hardly anyone around and everyone wearing masks, and sometimes rubber gloves as well.

Tuesday 10 August

SD rang. He says some people in his road have died. He claims to have seen people burying bodies in the back garden. I simply do not believe this. I told him that I didn't believe it, I said it's against the law to bury people in your garden, but he said it's true, it's what the Government had said to do, because of the hospitals not being able to cope any more. He is just exaggerating, as usual, blaming the Government for everything. We had quite a row about it. I know things are bad but why does he have to make them worse, saying things like that? It's like when he said about the aluminium and how we were

50

all going to go senile. Why does he want to scare people all the time? I suppose it's because he wants a revolution. Well, this is not the way to get one. He just turns you right against him.

Wednesday 11 August

SD didn't ring today. I expect he's mad at me for not believing him about the bodies. It turns out that it is right, what he said. I am trying not to think about it. *Families* still not back. Watched old film, *Breakfast at Tiffany's*. It was good. Wished Fran were here to watch it with me.

Thursday 12 August

Mum not feeling very well. I hope it's not the disease. I don't see how it can be, she has worn her mask all the time and not left the flat except for shopping and even then she didn't touch anyone. I tried to ring the doctor but all I got was his answering service. SD didn't ring again. I called some people from school but they must all be on holiday.

Friday 13 August

Mum very poorly. The doctor is still not there. I don't know what to do! I rang Fran's parents but they didn't answer and then I tried to ring Auntie Jen in Manchester just to talk to her, but the phone made funny buzzing noises and I couldn't get through and when I dialled the operator there was a recorded message saying there is a temporary fault on the line. After that I tried SD and some of the numbers in Mum's address book but the only person who answered was Mrs Andress who works in the shop. I'm sure it was Mrs Andress, I recognised her voice when she said hallo. But after she'd said hallo she didn't say any more. She just kept making these noises like gargling, it was horrible. I said, 'Mrs Andress, this is Harriet Somers. Please speak to me! Please say something,' and all she did was gargle so after a bit I got scared and put the receiver down and when I rang back a bit later nobody answered. I tried telling Mum about it, but I don't think she heard me. She looks terrible.

Saturday 14 August

Mum worse. Tried ringing all the doctors in the book one after another but only one answered, he was in Addiscombe. He asked me if I was mad and put the phone down. I have tried ringing the police but nobody answers. There is just a recorded message saying to stay indoors and listen to the news for the latest bulletins, but they don't say anything on the news, only that the epidemic still continues. What am I going to do?

Sunday 15 August

Mum says I am not to go into her room any more. She has made me promise. She says, 'By tomorrow it will all be over.' Watched television. *Dirty Harry, Little Women.* Cried in *Little Women.* Called to Mum when I went to bed but she didn't answer.

Monday 16 August

I am sleeping in the basement. I have put locks on the door. If the telephone rings I am not going to answer it. I am not going to write any more in this diary. This is THE END.

'The bright day is done; and we are for the dark.'

The rest of the pages were blank. Slowly Fran restored the diary to its hiding place beneath the duvet. Fancy Harry remembering that quotation from Shakespeare. It was ages since they had read *Antony and Cleopatra*; not since the fifth year. How pleased Mrs Dainty would be! She had always accused Harry of having a mind like a butterfly.

'Oh, Harry!'

Fran turned, and buried her face in Harry's shoulder. Harry, still asleep, rolled over to face her. They spent the night in each other's arms.

6

'But, Harry, we can't not eat!'

'People eat too much. That's why they're fat. I'm going to go and see what's on breakfast telly!'

Harry turned and went whisking off to the sitting room. Fran, resigned, paused just long enough to pour herself a handful of powered chocolate then went after her. Who knew? There might be some news. She had tried the radio down in the basement but the batteries had gone, and Harry, when applied to, had said she didn't know how to plug it into the mains, there wasn't any lead, or if there was it had long since been lost.

The radio in the kitchen seemed to have something wrong with it. VHF just crackled and spat, and most of the other frequencies emitted loud humming noises. There had been music, coming from a distance, faint and intermittent, and a voice which spoke in a foreign language which she couldn't understand, but nothing on Radio 4 or any of the local stations. She had said to Harry, 'Has it been like this for a long time?' but Harry didn't know. She didn't seem interested. All she wanted to do was try on dresses and look at the television.

The BBC was showing *The Sound of Music*. Harry had seen *The Sound of Music* at least twice already, but still she became quite irritable when Fran wanted to switch channels in search of news.

'What do you want news for? There isn't any news!'

'There's got to be some somewhere,' said Fran.

Harry sulked and said that even if there was it would only be boring. She said she wanted to watch *The Sound of Music*.

'It's my television, not yours. I'm the one that gets to choose.'

Fran felt like screaming. She felt like boxing Harry's ears. She felt, for a moment as if she were going mad. In the midst of disaster, they should sit and watch *The Sound of Music*?

'We have to know what's going on,' she said.

'I know what's going on.'

'What?' Fran faced her, challengingly. 'What *is* going on?'

Harry's bottom lip quivered. 'I don't want to talk about it. I just want to – '

'Well, you're not going to!' Fran lunged at the television, punching buttons for all she was worth before Harry could spring on her. She was just in time. As Harry's hand reached out they heard the words, '. . . pendent Television News bulletin' spoken in a strong Scots accent by a woman newsreader. Fran's fingers tightened over Harry's wrist.

'With the cordoning off of several of Britain's major cities yesterday, speculation is growing that the so-called London epidemic, thought so far to have been confined to the Greater London area, has now been identified in other parts of the country and may even have crossed the Channel and reached the French coast. Fears have been expressed that the epidemic may already be out of control and assuming the proportions of a global catastrophe. Government spokesmen, however, have strongly denied claims by the World Environment Defence Group that a germ warfare accident was responsible for setting off what WEDGE is calling "a megademic".

'A spokesman for the Prime Minister reiterated that yesterday's emergency move to isolate Britain's major cities was a purely precautionary measure intended to check any possible spread of the disease. He emphasised that while there was a need for people to remain vigilant, there was absolutely no cause for panic. The best advice remained, as it had always been: keep calm, use common sense, and follow the Government's Guidelines for Survival. He reminded people of what these guidelines were. Number

One' (the words appeared on the screen as the newsreader listed them:

No.1   Stay indoors as far as possible. DO NOT GO OUT UNLESS YOUR JOURNEY IS STRICTLY NECESSARY.
No.2   Boil all water used for drinking purposes.
No.3   If a member of your family becomes ill apply normal rules of hygiene and in addition use rubber gloves whenever you come into physical contact with the patient.
No.4   Incinerate all infected material.
No.5   Wear a mask at all times.

'If we all adhered to these simple guidelines, then the nation would pull through. The future, he said, was in our own hands. This is Bridget Matthews, Independent T – '

'*Stupid!*' Harry punched a vicious fist at the television, making the screen go blank and almost toppling the set on to the floor. 'Stupid, *stupid!*'

Fran sank back on to her heels. She thought, they didn't say anything about the bodies. About burying the bodies. 'Incinerate all infectious material.' Was a body infectious material? But how could you –

She ran a hand through her hair. Long, limp, listless. Mouse-coloured and wispy. Harry's, even now, was black and crisp, full of life and sparkle.

'It's all right,' said Fran. 'You can go back to your film.'

Harry pouted. 'I don't want to go back to the film. It's too late. I've missed all the best bits. Anyway, I've seen it. What do I want to see it again for? I've got better things to do than waste my time watching junk like that!'

In one swift movement, Harry was on her feet and headed for the door.

'Harry?' Fran, always less agile, scrambled up from the carpet and hurried after her. 'Where are you going?'

'I'm going to go and try on some dresses.'

'*Now?*'

'Why not?'

'Because – because, Harry, we have to talk! We have to decide – '

'Decide what?'

'What we're going to do! We can't just stay here like this, without eating. We've got to get out and get some food.'

'Food! Always food! You heard what they said . . . stay indoors!'

'As far as possible. They didn't say not go out at all. They said only go out if it's strictly necessary. Harry, this *is* necessary! We don't know how long it's going to be before – well! Before – '

Before what? Before help arrived? Before things got back to normal?

'It could be weeks. You can't live for weeks without food!'

'Yes, you can, I've done it. It's easy. Once you get used to it – '

'We are not going to starve ourselves to death,' said Fran. 'I don't care if it is easy. It would be cowardly.'

Last night, lying awake, muffling her tears in the pillow so as not to disturb Harry, Fran had spoken to Mum. Mum had whispered, 'We love you, darling. Be happy.' And Fran, through her tears, had whispered back, 'I will. I promise.' It was the only reason left for living: to be happy, for Mum's sake.

'If we go out there – ' Harry pointed, with trembling finger, towards the window ' – we'll die.'

'Yes, and if we stay here without food we'll die!'

'You don't know that! You're just saying it! People could come – '

'Which people?'

'*People*.'

'Where would they come from?'

'The Government! They'll organise things.'

'We don't even know if there still is a Government.'

'We do! They said!'

'Oh, Harry – ' Did she really believe what they told you on the television? The Government says, the Government does . . . 'Where *is* the Government?'

56

'Somewhere.'

'Where?'

'Somewhere secret.'

'Why secret? Why does it have to be secret? Why can't they say?' There was a silence. 'Why is it always Government *spokes*men? Why not the Prime Minister?' More silence. 'Harry, we can't afford to sit around waiting for something that may never happen! We need food . . . *now*.'

'We've got food! There's food here.' Harry darted across the hall into the kitchen. Frenziedly she began throwing open doors, hurling back the lid of the freezer, yanking open cutlery drawers, drawers full of towels, drawers full of tablecloths, scattering the contents, smashing crockery, in her frantic search for something that wasn't there. 'There is some! There's got to be!' Now she was down on her knees, in her crinoline, scrabbling amongst the mess of empty cans and cartons which littered the floor. 'Look! Look!' She leapt triumphantly to her feet, brandishing a tin beneath Fran's nose. 'I knew there was!'

Wearily, Fran took the tin from her. NAPOLINA, it said. TOMATO PUREE.

'It's food!' cried Harry.

'It's not enough.'

'There's rice! We could eat it with rice!'

'We ate the rice last night.'

Harry's face puckered. 'All of it?'

'There wasn't much.'

Harry sank back again on to the floor, the flounces of her crinoline spread out across the litter. Tears ran unrestrained down her cheeks.

'Oh, Harry!' Fran crouched beside her, encircling her with both arms. 'Don't be frightened . . . we'll be all right, now there's two of us. Things are always all right when we're together. Let's be brave and go now – right this minute!'

Harry looked up, tears still spilling from her eyes. 'Go where?'

'Back to my place. There's food there.' There were other things there, as well; but she wouldn't think of that. Not just at the moment. If she thought of that, she would never go. 'Come and put some other clothes on and let's do it quickly . . . get it over with.'

Harry let herself be led by the hand to her bedroom, she submitted to having a mask tied round her face (Fran had found one, discarded, on the table by the side of her bed) but she refused, with almost petulant, little-girl stubbornness, stamping her feet and vehemently shaking her head from side to side so that her curls bobbed and bounced like corkscrews, to be parted from the Victorian dress. Fran felt that she knew how mothers must feel when confronted with intransigent infants. Frustrated, she said, 'But, Harry, it's not practical!'

Harry flounced across the room. 'I don't want to be practical! I want to be useless and frivolous.' She gave a little twirl, flashing a roguish smile over her shoulder at her reflection in the dressing-table mirror. The crinoline hooped and spun. Harry kicked up a leg. She laughed. 'I could do the can-can!'

No sooner had the thought occurred to her than she was putting it into practice, all across the bedroom.

'I can-can, oh I ca-can, oh I ca-can, oh I can-can, *I* can-can, oh – '

Fran, with a sigh, went back to the kitchen to fetch a carrier bag. She knew from experience that Harry in one of her really determined moods of frivolity was quite unshakable. It had been funny, at school. It had driven some of the teachers crazy – it was the reason Mrs Dainty had accused her of having a mind like a butterfly. Of course everyone had encouraged her. When you were vivacious and pretty you could get away with things like that.

'If you don't want to change now – ' Fran dodged out of the way of a high kick ' – then we ought to take something with us.' She picked up a pair of denims and stuffed them into the bag. 'What else do you want? Shirts? Sweaters?'

Harry hunched a shoulder and sang. 'I don't care what I should wear, oh I don't care what I should wear – '

It was Fran who filled the bag with useful articles of

clothing. Harry just went on singing and kicking up her legs till she was red in the face and panting.

'Are you coming?' said Fran.

Harry put both hands to her waist, flopped over in the middle and hung, getting her breath back.

'Harry – '

'Oh, all *right*! Don't nag! I'm coming.'

Harry straightened up. She took a final glance at herself in the mirror, then followed Fran down the passage.

'Do you want – ' Fran hesitated, outside the closed door of Mrs Somers' bedroom. 'Do you want to – '

'What?'

'Do you want to say goodbye to your mum?'

Harry shouted, 'Goodbye, Mum!' To Fran she said, 'There. Do you think she heard me?'

Fran shook her head. 'I don't know.'

'Goodbye, Mum, where'er you be – ' Harry, grotesquely, had started again on her high kicks. 'Goodbye, Mum, where – '

'Harry! Please!'

'Oh, you're such a misery!' Harry stopped kicking and went rushing past Fran down the corridor. 'If we're going to go, then let's go!'

It was Fran who carried the bag containing Harry's clothes; but it was Harry who picked up the carving knife. She wouldn't put it in the bag.

'I'm keeping it with me,' she said.

Fran had a vague feeling that it was against the law to be in possession of an offensive weapon, but she didn't bother saying anything. She knew Harry wouldn't give it up, and anyway, what did it matter? Even if the law still existed, there wasn't going to be anyone around to enforce it.

7

Sajjad Khan was dead. He had died some time during the
night, while Shahid was lying on the sofa listening to the
radio. (The television still hadn't come back, but by going
all round the dial he had managed to find a radio station
that was still operating. It was churning out what Simon
called 'pop pap', all twanging guitars and swooning strings,
but anything was better than silence. Now and again a
voice would say something in what he was almost certain
was German. He couldn't understand it – though at one
point he caught the word *bacteriologische* followed by something which he thought might be World Environment Group
– but it was enough to know that there was someone out
there, still alive and talking.)

He could tell, as soon as he opened the door to his father's
room, that it was all over. There really wasn't any need to
go and check. He did so for form's sake – propitiating any
gods which might just happen to be watching – but a quick
glance was enough to confirm what he already knew.

He closed the bedroom door and went through to the
kitchen. There he boiled some water, made himself a cup of
black tea to assuage the worst of the hunger pangs – he had
finished off the last of the cans yesterday: chick peas in
salted water. It had made him feel quite nauseous – carefully examined the little finger of his right hand for signs of
infection (nothing, so far) and went back to the sitting room
to telephone Rahim.

'Shahid? What is happening?'

'I'm leaving,' said Shahid.

There was a silence.

'My father is dead?'

'He died during the night.'

'You were there?'

'Yes,' said Shahid.

'How was it for him? Was it peaceful?'

'Very peaceful.'

'He was in no pain?'

'No pain.'

'Did he say anything?'

'He commended me to your care.'

'Ah! So he could talk? I thought you said – '

'Just at the end. It was very faint.'

Rahim grunted. Shahid couldn't tell whether it was a grunt of disbelief or a grunt of satisfaction. (Was that really a slight redness on the inside of his little finger or was he imagining it?)

'So how are you going to get over here?'

'Walk.' He thought that on balance he was probably just imagining it. The light in the sitting room wasn't really reliable.

'How can you walk? It will take all day!'

'What else do you suggest?'

He couldn't drive, and even if he could he guessed it would be no use to him. The day before he got ill his father had tried going to the supermarket and had come back in a fury saying that someone had siphoned off all his petrol. He had instructed Shahid to take the spare can and go down to the local garage to fill up, but all the pumps at the local garage had either been empty or simply not functioning. Shahid had tramped the streets for over an hour looking for non-existent petrol. He had found some in the end but by the time he got back and his father had put it in the car and gone off to fill the tank all the shelves in the supermarket had been virtually cleared. (They had probably been cleared for days if the truth were known. It still hadn't stopped his father screaming at him that he was a useless oaf and an idiot.)

'Walking does not seem to me like a good idea.' Rahim

61

announced it in the considered tones of one who has deeply pondered the question. 'Is there no public transport?'

He must know very well that there wasn't. Who did he think was around to operate it? He was just looking for a way out. Any excuse for not getting into his own car and driving over. Rahim would have petrol: he would have made very sure of that.

'I'd come myself and pick you up,' said Rahim, 'but something has gone wrong with the car.'

Shahid smiled, politely, at the other end of the telephone. He didn't know why Rahim bothered. Who needed excuses? It was each man for himself. It always had been, of course, that was the philosophy the world lived by; but now more so than ever. There had only been one person Shahid would have risked his life for, and she was beyond the stage of needing sacrifices. He certainly wouldn't risk it for Rahim.

'Could you not perhaps – '

Perhaps what?

'I'll go and have a look at the bicycle shop in the High Street. Maybe I'll find something there.'

'You have the money?'

'Rahim,' said Shahid, 'if I had, who do you think would be there for me to give it to?'

A pause, while Rahim worked out the implications of this. 'I hope you are not saying – '

Yes; he was. 'If there's a machine there, I shall take it. If there isn't, I shall walk. Don't worry, I won't get lost, I've looked it up in the A-Z. If I don't make it by tonight I'll be with you in the morning. Just expect me when you see me.'

'And if you're not here by tonight? Where will you sleep?'

Shahid hunched a shoulder. The weather was warm, there were parks.

'Whatever you do,' said Rahim, 'don't talk to anyone. Keep well away from people.'

'I don't expect there'll be any people. Have you looked out of your windows lately?'

'To tell you the truth, we have all our windows boarded up. Planks, nailed across them.'

Of course; he might have known. People starved on the streets of Barnet while Siddiki & Khan put up the shutters and glutted on food sufficient for an army. Not that he blamed them. Who wouldn't, in their position? Only a saint, perhaps, or a fool.

'Believe me,' said Rahim, 'it was necessary. These people are like beasts – and the police, as usual, doing nothing. One has to take steps to defend one's property.'

'Oh, absolutely.' Shahid nodded, into the telephone. Couldn't agree more, old boy. A chap has to do what a chap has to do. All these damned wogs, looting and pillaging.

'What did you say?' said Rahim.

'I didn't say anything.'

'I thought you did.'

Not unless he was going mad. Which of course was quite possible. Twenty-four hours without the television, without John Wayne riding off into a thousand sunsets –

'Shahid? Are you all right?'

'Yes.' Shahid brought himself back with an effort. 'I'm fine. I'm going to pack a bag right now, then I'm going to call in at the restaurant – '

'Wouldn't that be dangerous? What do you want to call in at the restaurant for?'

'To see if I can find any food. Some of us out here have forgotten what it looks like.'

'Oh. Well, OK, but be careful. Stay away from trouble.'

Shahid replaced the telephone and went through to his bedroom. He stood for a moment, looking round. What, if anything, did he want to take? He would take his anorak, in case he had to spend the night in the open. His anorak had a hood; it also had pockets. He could fill the pockets with food from his father's restaurant, enough to keep him going for a couple of days. He would be with Rahim by then, and have all the food that anyone could desire.

Before leaving, he tried dialling Simon's number, but there wasn't any reply. There hadn't been, for almost two weeks now. There wasn't any from Julie's, either, but he thought there was just a chance that Julie might have got

63

away, right at the beginning. She had talked about an aunt and cousins she sometimes stayed with, up on the coast, in Lancashire. He hoped that was where she was, and not still in Croydon.

Automatically, as he went down the hall, he removed the front door key from its hook by the kitchen door. He looked at it a moment. What did he need the front door key for? Whatever happened, he wouldn't be coming back here again. But perhaps Rahim might want to. When it was all over. He might want to come back and . . . look. See for himself.

Shahid unzipped the inner pocket of his anorak and slid the key inside. There was something else in there. Something small, square, covered in cellophane . . . Durex Gold. Unopened. How many weeks ago was it that his mother had come across them, hidden in what he had thought was a safe place, on top of his wardrobe? Six weeks? Seven? (He had been so sure they would be safe on top of the wardrobe. His mother was only five foot nothing. What had she been *doing* up there?)

His mother hadn't know what Durex was. But she had suspected. She had asked him, gravely, if it was 'anything bad'. Useless trying to explain. Useless, subsequently, trying to convince his father that he was only acting like a responsible citizen. What Sajjad Khan had wanted to know was, *who did he think he was going to use them with*? No decent Muslim girl would go with him for that purpose.

Shahid and his father had had a truly appalling row. Sajjad Khan had shouted about prostitutes. To him, all white girls were prostitutes. They drank, they swore, they dressed improperly, they went with men. Shahid had objected to Julie being called a prostitute. He had yelled at his father that she was a virgin. How could you have a virgin who was a prostitute? His father had retorted that Shahid had no business knowing whether she was a virgin or whether she was not, and if that was what she had told him then it was obviously a lie. No right-minded girl would ever discuss such matters. He had demanded that Shahid

'give those evil things to me so that I may burn them.'
Shahid had refused. (He bet his father wouldn't have burned
them. Double standards was what that man had.)

He tucked the Durex back into his pocket along with the
front door key. You never knew when condoms might come
in handy . . . you could blow them up like balloons and tie
messages to them, or fill them with water, or roll them on
to your fingers and use them as fingerstalls. He didn't really
foresee any possibility of their being put to the purpose for
which they were intended. He remembered once reading a
book about World War Two which said that during times of
national peril people tended to get together far more readily
than ever they did in times of peace, but somehow he didn't
think it very likely that in the present situation many
people would fancy the idea. Making love in a mask . . . a
real turn-on that would be.

Carefully he shut the front door behind him. It was the
first time he had ventured outside since the day he had been
sent to get petrol. He walked along the corridor, with its
bare concrete floor and whitewashed walls, to the lift. The
doors of all the other flats were closed. No milk bottles stood
on the mats, no local freebies, no *Comets* or *Posts*, stuck
through the letter-boxes. The lift seemed not to be working.
The lights flashed and machinery whirred, but nothing
actually happened. He walked down to the next floor and
discovered why: a body was jammed in the half-open door.
He didn't hang around trying to identify it. It looked as if it
had been there some time.

Shahid pressed a handkerchief over his mask and continued on his way down. Somewhere on the third floor he heard
what sounded like a baby crying. He hesitated. Walked a
short way along the corridor. Listened.

The crying stopped. Either there was someone still there,
looking after the child, or –

Or there wasn't.

He turned, ran back to the stairwell and went hurtling
down, flinging himself from one flight to the next, taking
the corners at a speed almost suicidal in his sudden frantic

desire to be out of the place. If the crying came again, at least he wouldn't be around to hear it.

Outside, the sun was shining. The air, after the rancid odours of the flats, smelt fresh and sweet. With no traffic fumes to poison it, it possibly was so. And there again, possibly was not so. The Government didn't go round dishing out free masks for nothing.

He didn't care. He stood, face uplifted to the blue skies, gulping in great mouthfuls. The effect was almost intoxicating.

Harry and Fran didn't meet anyone as they walked down the High Street. Nevertheless they pressed close to each other, keeping instinctively to the middle of the road.

'Shall we go up the hill?' said Fran, 'Or – '

She looked at Harry, seeking guidance. Harry clutched at her knife, half-hidden within the folds of the tartan skirt.

'Why not?'

They always went back up the hill; up the hill and through the Flats. It cut the journey almost in half. Yesterday, on her way down, Fran had taken that route without even thinking about it. This morning –

'Do you think we ought?' she said.

Harry tossed her head. For just a moment she was the old, defiant, fearless Harry that Fran had always known.

'I'm not going miles out of my way!' she said.

They set off up the hill, where once there had been cherry orchards and now were 1930's semis and blocks of council flats. Halfway up, on the left, was the block officially known as Alton Court. A great grey looming tenement, straddling the neighbourhood on concrete stilts above a deep, slab-sided embankment.

Harry turned in without hesitation. Fran, who might even now have retraced her steps, had no choice but to follow. Together they picked their way across the lumpy cobbles which the Council had planted in place of grass. Harry, in her flat slippers, trod warily on tiptoe. Fran still had on her trainers from camp; the cobbles didn't bother her.

As they skirted the edge of the building, a scraping sound came from out of the darkness beneath the concrete stilts. Harry froze.

'What was that?'

'N-nothing. Rats, probably.' Fran gave a little nudge forward. 'Let's – '

Before she could finish, a small masked face had appeared over the edge of the embankment. A pair of hands clung. A pair of eyes glittered. Another face appeared, and then another. Harry screamed. For a moment Fran wanted to scream as well. She forced herself to keep calm: they were only little boys. They came swarming over the top, half a dozen in all. None could have been more than about ten years old, the youngest no more than four or five.

'What you got in there, lady?' One of them pointed to the bag which Fran carried.

'Nothing that would interest you,' said Fran.

'You got food in there?'

'No. No food.'

'What, then?' The gang surrounded them, six little boys, full of menace. 'What you got in there?'

'None of your business,' said Fran. Just in time, she swung the bag over her head, out of their reach. The tallest of them made a snatch at it as it flew past. At the same moment the tiniest one, in a movement too well rehearsed to be spontaneous, dived for Fran's legs, hurling his arms about her. She would have gone down had it not been for Harry.

Harry and her kitchen knife.

Fran had a brief glimpse of steel flashing in the sun; and this time she did scream.

8

'It was a kid! Just a kid!' Shahid had thought he was beyond the stage of being shocked. Kids, after all, were dying all the time. Babies cried in empty flats, starving toddlers wailed at windows. Why shed tears over just one more? Because it would have been uncalled-for, that was why. He let go the girl's arm and bent to pick up the discarded knife. She glared at him, insolently, dark eyes a-glitter with something which looked very much like hate. Harriet Somers. She had always been a nut-case. Pretty, but bananas. Hyperactive was what they called it nowadays. Hyper-raving-potty if you asked him.

'You could have had a murder on your conscience,' he said.

'It wasn't Harry's fault!' The other girl was swift to defend her. As always. Fran Latimer and Harriet Somers were a twosome so tight you couldn't get a wedge between them. Brett Forrester, who reckoned he knew all there was to know about the female sex, had written them off as a couple of dykes, though Simon had said that was typical of Brett Forrester: 'Big macho pig talk. Just because they're not falling over themselves.' No, well, just at this moment Shahid wasn't falling over himself, either.

'She couldn't help it.' Fran placed a protective arm round Harriet's thin shoulders. 'They came at us.'

'Kids!' he said. 'Just a bunch of little kids!'

'There were older ones . . . there were lots of them. She was frightened.'

Weren't they all?

'I suppose it didn't occur to you,' he said, 'that they were probably far more frightened than you?'

Fran's lower lip quivered. He could see the puckering of her mask.

'They're probably starving. They probably haven't eaten for days. Their parents are probably dead. They've got no one to turn to. Nowhere to go.' Now that he had started, he found it difficult to stop. 'Kids!' he said. 'Little kids! And they've had to live through all this . . . they've had to watch their mothers – their fathers – sisters, brothers, grand-mothers – everyone! Until there was just them.'

At least, thank God, that had not happened to Roshana.

'Did you – know them?' said Fran.

He didn't have to know them. Though come to think of it, he believed they probably were from the Flats. Some of the little hooligans his father was forever on about. Maybe even the ones who had syphoned off his precious petrol.

Fran hooked her hair back over her ears. Her hands were trembling.

'Please,' she whispered, 'please don't get mad at Harry.'

The anger which had flared in him had already evapor-ated. What right had he, who left babies crying in flats, to pass judgement on some poor crazy girl for carrying a knife around? Everyone knew that Harriet Somers was off the wall. Old Loopy Loo they'd called her at school. The boys, mainly, but some of the girls as well. She stood there now, playing with her crinoline (what the hell was she wearing a crinoline for? That showed she was out of her tree) for all the world as if the incident of a few seconds ago had never occurred; or if it had, was no concern of hers.

'It was my fault.' Fran said it desolately. The tears spilled over from eyes that were pale-lashed and only very faintly washed with colour. She had always reminded Shahid of an angora rabbit. 'Harry didn't want to come in the first place. I was the one that made her. I should have listened to her . . . she said not to do it.'

'So where are you headed? Anywhere in particular?'

Fran smeared the back of her hand across her eyes. 'We were on our way home,' she said.

'Your home?' He remembered, now; she lived somewhere

quite close. They had occasionally caught the same bus into school, getting on at the same stop. He remembered something else. 'I thought you were away? At that place – that camp?'

'It finished.'

'And they let you come back?'

'Nobody knew. We didn't have any newspapers or – or radios or anything.'

She was crying again. He wished he could stretch out a hand to comfort her, but one didn't do that sort of thing any more; not these days. Touching as a way of life was definitely out.

'It wasn't till I – till I got home and – ' She pushed again at her hair, agitatedly looping it back over her ears with the index fingers of both hands. 'Mum had – left – this note. She'd written it – for me – then she'd – gone upstairs – to be – with – Dad.' She pressed a hand, inelegantly, to her mask, making a snuffling sound. Shahid felt for her: tears were difficult to cope with, when you were wearing a mask. 'I spent the night with Harry. It's been awful for her. She's been – all alone. That's – why – '

Why she was loopy. Why she ran around with carving knives. Why she stood there, now, jiggling about and pleating the folds of her dress.

'She's been on her own, all this time, with her – with her mother – '

'I thought you said she was on her own?'

'Her mother has – been dead – ' Fran's voice broke. 'Days ago – and she's – been there – by herself – and these – telephone – calls – and this – man – keeps r-ringing – making s-suggestions – '

Shahid, after a polite pause, in case there might be something more, said, 'Way out.'

Fran's head jerked up. There was hurt in her eyes. 'It's been horrible for her!'

'Like I said . . . way out.' The rest of them had had a ball.

For a moment she was angry. And then the penny dropped; she understood.

'I'm sorry. It must have – been the same – for everyone.

It's just – ' She drew in her breath. 'It's just that I – haven't – got used to it – yet.'

'It doesn't take long. The worst thing is, all the social conventions have gone. You meet someone in the street, like I meet you, for instance, and you don't know what to say . . . "Hallo, there! Lovely weather for the time of year. Been on holiday yet?" What we need is something new, like . . . "Still around, I see?" And then when you say goodbye you could say, "Have a good dying, now!"'

Too late, he remembered: a sense of humour had never been one of her strong points. He remembered once in class, when they'd had to read poems of their own choosing, Brett Forrester had read *It was the good ship Venus, by God, you should have seen us!* Fran had sat there looking as if she had a prune in her mouth. Not that she had been the only one, old Loopy and some of the other girls had been just as bad. But that had been vulgar humour. Coarse, some might have said. This wasn't vulgar, this was sick. Have a good dying, now! He was quite proud of that one. Sick humour to go with a sick world. What was wrong with that?

Everything, it seemed. Fran's eyes looked at him accusingly over her mask. She turned, without a word, and went to rejoin Harriet.

'Harry?' She slid a comforting arm about her waist. She obviously didn't mind touching. 'It's all right. It's all over.'

He felt like shouting, 'What do you mean, it's all over? It's hardly even begun!' Instead, holding out the knife, he said, 'Hadn't you better take this? You might have need of it.'

She turned, frowning; obviously suspecting him of sarcasm.

'I mean it,' said Shahid.

Reluctantly, she accepted it from him. Harriet, doing little swirls all by herself on the pavement, had started to sing. For a moment nobody spoke; then at the same time as Fran opened her mouth, Shahid did likewise.

'What – '

They stopped, simultaneously.

71

'Sorry,' said Shahid.

'After you,' said Fran.

'I was just going to ask you . . . what you were going back home for? I mean – ' If there was nobody there, then what was the point?

'We were going to find something to eat,' said Fran.

'We have things to eat at my father's restaurant.'

There was a pause. Harriet twirled and chirruped.

'As a matter of fact,' said Shahid, 'that's where I'm headed right now. You could come with me, if you wanted.'

Fran hesitated. She looked at Harriet, but Harriet was busy singing to herself – 'I can-can, oh I can-can, oh I can-can, oh I can-can' – doing little jigging motions with her feet in time to the music. It was a moot point, if you asked Shahid, whether she was any more loopy now than she had been before. She had *always* been loopy. But she was Fran's mate. If he wanted the company of the one, he would have to put up with the other.

'You'd like to come to my father's restaurant, wouldn't you?' He spoke directly to Harriet for the first time.

She looked up at him and beamed. '*I* would like to come with you, oh I would like to come with you, *I* would like, oh *I* would like, oh I would – '

'All right,' said Fran. 'We'll come.'

Fran had never really had that much to do with Shahid Khan at school. If anyone had asked her she would probably have described him as being arrogant and pushy, though looking back she couldn't remember ever having exchanged more than half a dozen words with him in all the time they had been there.

She knew, of course, that he lived in the Flats. Sometimes they had waited at the same bus-stop in the mornings, and Fran had always smiled and nodded before immersing herself in a book or frowning over a piece of homework, in order to avoid having to talk. Talking was such an embarrassment; she never knew what to say. It was easy for people like Harry. They could just open their mouths and burble, and everyone laughed and found them amusing. If Fran ever tried burbling people just stared at her as if she were mad.

She had known that the Khans had a restaurant because Harry, who always knew everything about everyone, had once pointed it out to her. She had never been in there – Mum and Dad weren't the sort to go out, except on anniversaries, and then it was usually a Berni Inn or the Steak House. Dad wouldn't have liked Indian food. He was very conservative.

'What shall we have?' said Harry. She did a little skip as they went back down the hill. 'Do you do onion bhajis?'

'Yes,' said Shahid. He looked at Fran over the top of Harry's head. Fran, deliberately, looked the other way. She wasn't entering into an alliance with him against Harry.

'I shall have one onion bhaji,' said Harry, 'and one poppadam. One of the spicy ones. Do you do the spicy ones?'

'Yes,' said Shahid. 'We do everything.'

'You can't do *every*thing.'

'Almost everything.'

'Fruit juice?'

'We do fruit juice.'

'What fruit juice?'

'Pineapple fruit juice, orange fruit juice, grapefruit fruit juice, tom – '

'Passion fruit juice? I bet you don't do passion fruit juice!'

'No,' said Shahid. He said it in the patronising tone of one who humours a young child. 'We don't do that.'

Harry turned, triumphant, to Fran. 'I knew they wouldn't! *N*obody does passion fruit juice. I knew I'd catch him out!'

Fran smiled, and squeezed her hand.

'I think maybe I'll just have a Perrier water,' said Harry. 'I don't want to get fat.'

Shahid looked at her; then looked again at Fran. 'How long is it since you had anything?'

'I had something only yesterday.' (Had it really been yesterday that Fran had eaten a normal hearty breakfast at

73

camp? It seemed a lifetime ago.) 'It's Harry who's gone without. She's the one who really needs something.'

'No, I don't,' said Harry. 'I'm *fat*.'

Shahid ignored that. He spoke directly to Fran, over Harry's head. 'When we get there I could make you a curry if you like.'

'Curry for *break*fast?' said Harry.

'You can have curry at any time of day.'

'*I* shan't have curry. I shall have – '

'Perrier water,' said Shahid. 'We know.'

They reached the bottom of the hill and turned right, into the Brighton Road.

'There,' said Shahid. He pointed ahead. The restaurant was sandwiched between a large DIY store and an office equipment shop. On the pavement stood a brightly-coloured model of the Taj Mahal and a sign which said 'Tandoori Restaurant'. A large plastic tub, outside the DIY, was still filled with rolls of wallpaper. It all looked so normal.

'I'll go round the back,' said Shahid. 'You two wait at the front, I'll come and let you in.'

Shahid peeled off, down a narrow passage which ran by the side of the shops. Fran and Harry walked on, past the extended frontage of the DIY. As they approached the Taj Mahal they could see shards of glass glistening on the pavement. Harry, in her flimsy slippers, hopped out into the gutter. She darted forward.

'What's happened?' Fran hurried after her, trainers scrunching on the glass. 'Oh, no!'

It was what you read about. What you saw on the television, after riots and disasters. She said again, 'Oh, *no*!'

Harry sniffed, contemptuously. 'Him and his big ideas . . . well, that's curry out the way!'

Fran looked at her, reproachful; hurt, on Shahid's behalf. 'He was only trying to help.'

'Showing off.' Harry minced, swishing her crinoline in the gutter. '*My father's restaurant* . . . I don't know why we came here with him anyway. I thought we were going back to your place?'

'I thought you wanted to come here?'

74

'*I* didn't want to come here! What would I want to come here for? Let's go!' Harry caught at Fran's arm, trying to tug her back up the road. 'Quick, before he comes!'

'Harry, don't – ' Fran pulled away. 'We can't do that. It's mean!'

'Well, he's mean! I hate him! He told Simon Dobson I was neurotic.'

'One shouldn't bear grudges,' said Fran.

'You'd bear grudges! If I told you what he said about you . . . do you want to know what he said about you? He said – '

'I don't want to know!'

'He said you were pasty-faced!'

Fran swallowed. 'Well, he's probably right.'

'He's not right! It's a hateful thing to say.'

'I don't see that it matters very much . . . *now*.'

'It matters to me! I hate him for it!'

'Oh, Harry,' cried Fran, 'do stop!'

Impatient, in spite of herself – Harry *could* be trying – she stepped across the broken glass towards the devastation that had been the Taj Mahal. (Pasty-faced. That was more than just being pale. Pasty meant all lumpy and puffy.) Through the jagged hole in the window she could see all the lovely gold chairs with their pink velvet upholstery lying on their sides, backs broken, legs snapped like twigs. She could see broken bottles, spilling their contents over the rose-coloured carpet, and strips of crimson wallpaper hanging from the walls.

Shahid appeared, from a door at the far end. He stood for a moment, taking it in. Watching him, Fran remembered the man in evening dress whom she had seen when Harry had originally pointed the restaurant out to her. He had been standing in the doorway, tall and stern-looking, with a brooding scowl. She had thought at the time that he was probably the head waiter. Now she realised that he must have been Shahid's father. She had suddenly seen the likeness.

She watched as Shahid picked his way towards them

through the ruins. He unlocked the door and stepped through on to the pavement. There was a silence; then Shahid hunched his shoulders.

'It seems I dragged you all this way for nothing.'

Fran shook her head; sympathetic, not knowing what to say.

'What about my Perrier water?' Harry's voice was querulous. 'I thought I was supposed to be getting a Perrier water?'

Shahid stepped back a pace. He gestured. 'If you can find a Perrier water in there, you're welcome.'

'So now what do we do? We come all this way – '

'Harry, don't,' said Fran. She looked across at Shahid. 'There's food in my place,' she said. 'At least . . . there was. If nobody's – got to it.'

'All right,' said Shahid. He swung round. 'We'll go to your place.'

Fran felt Harry's fingers digging into her arm as they walked back together, the way they had come. She knew Harry didn't want Shahid to be with them. She knew she was resenting it. But what could you do? You couldn't just ignore people. He hadn't ignored them. And anyway, there was safety in numbers.

Halfway up the hill they reached the Flats. Shahid turned in, automatically. Both Fran and Harry came to a full stop. He looked back at them, eyebrows raised.

'Isn't this the way you go? Well, come on, then! What are you waiting for?'

He jerked his head, authoritatively. Fran remembered, at school, he had always had a tendency to be assertive. Bossy was what Harry had called it. Meekly, as there was no alternative, Fran set off after him across the cobbles. Harry trailed, a few paces behind.

'You don't have to worry,' said Shahid. 'They won't do anything if I'm with you. They were only little kids, after all.'

'So what if they were?' The words came shrieking, sudden and shrill, from Harry. 'What would it have mattered? What

76

does any of it matter? You don't have to look at me like that! I'm not mad! I know what's going on . . . we'd all of us be better dead!'

There was a long silence; then Shahid, grimly, said: 'I expect, very soon, we all shall be.'

9

'Of course, there is another way,' said Shahid.

Both girls stopped eating and looked at him. They were sitting in Fran's back garden, in the shade of an apple tree on the sunbaked grass. They had made a picnic and taken it outside. Outside had a strange, surrealistic quality – a stillness and a quiet that was almost total: not a dog that barked, not a leaf that stirred: not even planes in the sky overhead – but inside was enough to make your flesh crawl. They had headed instinctively for the open air.

'There is always an alternative,' said Shahid.

'What?' It was Fran who asked the question. She didn't make it sound antagonistic as Harriet would. Harriet, for some reason, seemed to hate him.

'Well . . . if we could get out the way you got in – '

'Through the houses?' She sounded doubtful.

'Why not?' It was obvious, now he stopped to think about it. 'Assuming no one's blocked it off.'

She still seemed doubtful.

'They'd shoot us,' said Harriet.

'Who would? There wasn't anyone about. Was there?' He glanced across at Fran for confirmation. She shook her head.

'I thought you said there was a woman and some children? I thought you s – '

'Women and children do not shoot people. Soldiers shoot people. There are no soldiers,' said Shahid, 'over the allotments.'

'How do you know? There could be by now.'

'So, all right, there could be! So I'll go first. That way, if anyone's going to get shot it'll be me.' That would please her. He had the feeling she would be only too happy to see

78

the back of him. He couldn't think what he had ever done to
annoy her, but maybe with people like Harriet you didn't
have to do things. He had probably failed to notice her one
day, or stepped on her toe and not apologised. He looked
again at Fran. 'What do you reckon?'

'The thing is . . . where would we go?'

'Once we were out?'

'Yes. I mean – we'd have to go *some*where.'

'I have family in Birmingham.' Najda's uncle lived in
Birmingham. He was family; sort of. He would let them
stay. It was just a question of making their way up there.
'There might still be the odd train.'

'Not to Birmingham.' Harriet, busy chopping her peach
halves into peach quarters, announced it with an air of flat
finality: that had put paid to *that*. 'Nothing's going to
Birmingham. It's been shut off.'

'Birmingham has?' That shook him. It was the first he'd
heard of it. '*Birmingham's* been shut off?'

'And Leeds. *And* Liverpool. *And* Manchester. *And* Glas-
gow. *And* Edinburgh. *And* – '

'It was on the news,' said Fran. She said it apologetically;
as if in some way it was her fault. 'All the big cities.'

'Cardiff. Bristol. S – '

'Just as a precaution,' said Fran. 'At least . . . that's what
they said.'

'To stop it spreading.' The peaches, by now, had been
chopped into sixteenths. 'To stop people travelling. It only
makes sense. That's why – ' with her fork, Harriet began on
a mashing job ' – why we all ought to do what they say and
stay indoors.'

'Stay indoors and die,' said Shahid. 'Like rats in a trap.'

There was a silence. Harriet mashed her peaches. Fran
sat frowning, cross-legged, plucking at the parched grass.

'My grandmother lives down in Cornwall,' she said.

'*Corn*wall? We can't go to Cornwall!' Harriet smashed her
fork down on top of her battered peaches. A spray of peach
juice splattered into Shahid's face.

'Even if we could – ' Fran hooked her hair behind her

ears. 'Suppose we're – well, infectious. We might go and give it to people.'

He looked at her, broodingly. He wasn't at all convinced that it mattered, whether or not you were infectious. Simon had had a theory that anything which could spread so fast had to be airborne. He had said the Government weren't telling the truth about it. If Simon were right, which he probably was – he was pretty sharp, was Simon; pretty much on the ball. He knew what he was talking about. So if Simon were right, it really didn't make much difference whether they stayed or whether they went. They were probably going to die, whichever they did. He had just thought that perhaps, maybe, getting out of London would have given them a faint chance. But what the hell.

He wiped his arm across his face, where the peach juice had splashed him.

'In that case, we'd better stick to my original plan . . . we'll go to my brother's.'

'All of us?' said Fran.

'Well, you can't stay here. Not on your own.' Besides, now that he had found company, he was loath to give it up. 'The fun's hardly started yet. When it does, you won't want to be by yourselves.'

'But what will your brother say?'

Rahim wouldn't say anything. He couldn't: he was family. If Shahid turned up with people who had placed themselves under his protection, then Rahim was duty bound to take them in. Just as Shahid had been duty bound to stay with his father.

'Rahim is my brother,' said Shahid. 'My friends are his friends. He'll make you welcome.' He stood up. 'If we're going to go, then I think we should go soon. I said I'd try and get there tonight.'

'Where does he live?' Fran, already, was starting to clear the remains of the picnic, stacking dishes on the tray. He wondered why she bothered. She was obviously one of those people with a naturally tidy mind.

'He lives in Barnet.'

'Barnet?' She sat back, looking startled. 'Isn't that rather a long way?'

'North London.' Within the confines; just. Rahim had been furious, as if it were some kind of personal vendetta. 'Why Barnet?' he'd kept saying. 'Why Barnet? Another couple of miles and we would have been all right!' Another couple of miles and they would have been on the other side of the barricades. It was exactly the same for those in Croydon, but Rahim hadn't seemed to care about that.

'How will we get there?' Fran sounded worried. 'Will the tubes be running?'

He reminded himself that she had spent the past four weeks living in the Stone Age.

'Nothing's running. Public transport packed up almost right at the beginning. There might be a bike or two lying around if we're lucky. If not, we'll just have to walk. *She'll* need to change.' He jerked his head at Harriet, still mushing around with her fork in her dish of peaches. 'She can't go like that.'

'No.' Fran looked at her, warily. 'We did bring some other clothes with us . . . Harry, aren't you going to eat that?'

'I'm full,' said Harriet. 'I'll burst if I eat any more.'

Fran and Shahid exchanged glances.

'You'll need to get your strength up,' said Shahid, 'if you're going to walk to Barnet.'

'Barnet?' Fear and suspicion flashed into Harriet's eyes. He noticed, for the first time, that they were deep blue. He had always thought they were black. 'What are we going to Barnet for?'

'We're going to stay with Shahid's brother.'

'What for?'

'Because we can't stay here by ourselves,' said Fran. 'We need to be with people.'

'Why? I don't want to be with people! I want to stay here! Why can't we stay here?'

'I'll tell you why,' said Shahid. He squatted before her, talking directly at her as if she were a child. 'This business is only at the beginning. It's going to get a whole lot worse

81

before it gets any better.' If it ever did get any better, which privately he doubted. 'There's going to be a shortage of food, for a start. And when there's a shortage of food, people get desperate. And when people get desperate, they get nasty. Like that gang of little kids – except that it won't always be little kids. One day it'll be big kids. And then what are you going to do?'

She shrank from him. 'We'll stay indoors, like they told us! We'll barricade ourselves in!'

'And when the food runs out?'

'It won't run out! There's cupboardfuls of it!'

'Cupboardfuls!' He laughed, derisively. 'Enough to last two weeks if you're lucky – three at a stretch. That's if you're allowed to keep it. If the mob don't break in and murder you for it.'

'They won't be able to! We'll go back to my place – we'll go down the basement!'

'And live like mushrooms in the dark!'

'It isn't dark! Tell him!' She turned, frantically, to Fran. 'We've got a light down there! We've got everything!'

Gently, Fran said: 'We haven't got food.'

'We'll take some! We'll take some with us!'

'But, Harry, we can't live in the basement for – for however long it's going to be!'

'A long time,' said Shahid. 'Believe me.'

'How does *he* know? He doesn't know any more than we do!'

'Common sense,' he said. 'They're not going to clear this lot up overnight.' It might be that they were never going to clear it up at all. One had to be prepared for the thought that the world might actually be approaching Armageddon.

'Shahid's right,' said Fran. 'It could be months.'

'It could be for ever.'

She shot him a scared glance.

'Face facts,' said Shahid.

'What *facts*?' Harriet challenged him. 'Going on about *facts*. What do you know?'

'You want to know what I know? I'll tell you what I know!' He stabbed a finger in her face. 'I know that almost all of my family are dead: I know that most of the people I have ever known are dead: I know that society has ceased to function ... no hospitals, no doctors, no police ... no transport, no broadcasting ... no newspapers ... no heating, no lighting ... even in wartime, that doesn't happen. But it's happened now. This time they've really done it. So don't ask me what I know! I know what you know, and if you don't know it's the end – '

'*We* have lighting,' said Harriet. 'And we have heating.'

'So how the hell long do you think that's going to last?'

He screamed it at her, across the stillness of the garden. Harriet tossed her head and made a little huffing noise. With her fork she held up dribbling streams of peach juice and fibre. There was a silence.

'Don't play with it,' said Fran. 'If you don't want it – '

'I don't want it!'

With sudden savagery, Harriet hurled both dish and fork into a nearby flower-bed. Fran stood, holding her tray.

'That was a waste,' said Shahid.

'It was mine to waste if I wanted!'

He shrugged.

'Your brother,' said Fran. 'Shouldn't we – ' she gestured, with the tray ' – take something with us?'

'If you mean food, he has all the food he could want. He stocks the stuff.'

'You mean he has a *shop*,' said Harriet.

'Better than a shop; it's a wholesalers. He doesn't need any more. We'll just take enough to keep us going, in case we have to stop off overnight.' They left Harriet in the garden and went back into the house to start preparing.

There was a rucksack in the kitchen, with the sleeping-bag which had gone with Fran to camp. They discussed whether to take the sleeping-bag or leave it. Shahid was for leaving it, but Fran was worried they might have to spend the night out of doors. (She didn't say it was Harriet she was worried about, but he bet he knew which of them would get to sleep in it should the occasion arise.) He gave way on the sleeping-bag, since it seemed so important to her.

'But it's only about twenty miles. There's no reason we shouldn't do it in one day if we really step out.' Fran looked fit enough, and one thing about Loopy, she had always been athletic. He remembered seeing her play netball, flashing up and down the court in her green school shorts and white trainers. Twenty miles wasn't really anything.

'What about clothes?' Fran said it rather timidly, obviously feeling guilt over the sleeping-bag.

'I'm not bothering,' he said, 'but I suppose you ought to take a few basics.'

'I'll just take what I've got here.' Quickly she upended the rucksack and transferred the contents – pants, T-shirts, sponge bag, paper handkerchiefs, spare pair of jeans – to a carrier bag. He gathered Harriet's junk was in the carrier bag she had had with her that morning. In which case, why hadn't it been Harriet who was carrying it? Was the girl totally useless?

He picked up the rucksack and set it on the kitchen table. 'We can use this for the food.'

It was going to have to be mainly tins. Fran had been dismayed, on looking into the refrigerator earlier, to find that all the milk had gone off, that the butter was rancid, the cheese hard and yellow. Shahid had pointed out that in view of the weather it was hardly very surprising, but Fran had shaken her head in evident distress, upset out of all proportion, or so it had seemed to him.

'It's not like Mum! She would never have left things.'

What did she expect? That a dying woman would stop to clear the refrigerator? Now, opening it again as they filled the rucksack, she said: 'I expect what it was, she was thinking of me . . . in case I got back and wanted something. She wouldn't have known it was going to be like this.'

'That's right,' said Shahid, anxious that she should be happy. 'Nobody said anything about a heat wave.'

'She threw the bread away.' She indicated an upturned bread bin. She seemed more at peace now that she had found a satisfactory explanation for all the stuff going mouldy in the fridge. She took out a carton of milk, opened it, and poured the contents down the sink. He watched her, disbelieving.

'What are you doing?'

A tinge of pink crept into her cheek. 'I can't leave it like this . . . Mum would have hated it.'

Her voice pleaded: she obviously knew she was being ridiculous. He shrugged his shoulders and left her to it. Everyone had their own hang-ups. He wasn't sure what his were – watching television was one, perhaps. If the set hadn't gone on the blink he might have been sat there even now, glued to the screen. At least Fran was still relatively sane, unlike old Loopy out there. He watched her for a moment through the kitchen window. She was kneeling, upright, with the flounces of her skirt spread all about her. That would have to go. He wasn't parading the streets with some nutter in a crinoline.

He turned, and became aware that Fran was now filling the sink with water. She was actually preparing to wash up. This was too much! One loopy female he could stand; not two. Stretching across, he flipped out the plug.

'We haven't got time for all that!' What did she think it was, the start of a holiday?

She looked at him, hurt. 'Mum made time. It was clean when we came.'

Maybe it was. So what? He hardened his heart. He had let her get away with the sleeping-bag, he had let her empty the fridge. Enough was enough. He drew the line at washing up. She'd be down on her knees scrubbing the floor before he knew it.

'Let's get this rucksack filled.' He reached into the cupboard and took out a couple of cans of soup. 'Have you got a tin-opener?'

'I'll get one.'

She was all right once she had something positive to do. She still had a bit of a fetish about not arriving empty-handed – left to herself, she would have filled the rucksack to the brim – but he stood firm. Rahim had more food than he knew what to do with, and besides, who was going to carry the thing?

'Oh, I'll carry it!' she said. 'After all, it's my rucksack.'

'Don't be daft,' he said.

The pink came back into her cheeks. 'I carried it all the way from Purley!'

'Not with half a hundredweight of tins in it. If you want to fill the last few inches, let's take something useful . . . a blanket, or something. Do you have a blanket?'

She twisted a strand of hair round a finger. 'There's one upstairs.'

'Tell me where,' said Shahid, 'and I'll get it.'

'It's in my – bedroom. It's the door on the – right, at the top of the stairs.'

'Anything else you want while I'm up there?' She shook her head. 'OK. You hang on.'

Her bedroom was as he would have pictured it, if he were ever to have set himself the task: pastel pink wallpaper, in Regency stripe, gloss white windows and skirting board. Everything gleamingly clean and neat. Big colour posters of the pop group Save the World on one wall: postcard-size repros of French Impressionists (Manet, Monet? He wasn't really into art) on another. Rows of books, probably in alphabetical order. Uncluttered dressing-table with a bean-frog sitting on it. Glass shelf full of china knick-knacks. Pink candlewick on the bed.

He pulled back the candlewick and yanked off a blanket. Funny, not having a duvet. He'd thought everyone had duvets these days. Even his dad hadn't found anything to object to in a duvet. Maybe Fran's parents had been old-fashioned.

He glanced at the closed door of the room next to hers. Only glanced, because Fran was at the foot of the stairs, watching him.

'OK?' he said.

She nodded. They went back to the kitchen, folded the blanket and squashed it in at the top of the rucksack.

'What about her?' He jerked a thumb in the direction of

86

Harriet, no longer kneeling upright but sunk down, like some exotic flower, into the swirling billows of her skirt.

'I'll get her.'

'What about the clothes? She can't come like that.'

'No, I'll – I'll talk to her.'

'Why talk to her? Just *tell*.'

He turned back into the kitchen. There was a drawer next to the sink where all the kitchen implements were kept. He had seen them when Fran had gone there to get the tin-opener. Keeping one eye on the garden, he slid it open, picked out the smallest and sharpest knife he could find, wrapped a sheet of kitchen roll round the blade and eased it into the back pocket of his jeans. Old Loopy Loo might be round the twist, and no way was he letting her loose again with a deadly weapon – he wouldn't fancy his chances too much, some of the looks she gave him – but to set out with no means of protection at all would seem to be asking for trouble.

He moved back again to the window. Harriet, still kneeling in her froth of tartan, was throwing her head about, tossing it violently from side to side like a child in a tantrum. Fran had a look of desperation on her face. Too soft, that was her trouble. It wasn't any use trying to reason with spoilt brats like Harriet.

As he watched, the spoilt brat suddenly flounced to its feet. It evidently had no intention of doing anything it didn't want to do. Shahid threw open the back door and strode out into the heat. The two girls were coming towards him across the grass, Fran leading Harriet. Harriet raised her head and looked at him. It was a look of sheer malevolence. Fran, quickly forestalling him, said: 'Harry would rather stay as she is for the moment. We've got a change of clothes if she wants to put them on later.'

He opened his mouth; and then, seeing Fran's expression, closed it again. Harriet was her mate, let her deal with her.

'So are we ready?'

'Yes.' Fran hooked her hair back. 'We can go now.'

Shahid shouldered the rucksack, Fran took the carrier bags. Harriet, typically, went empty-handed.

As they left the house, Fran hesitated.

'You don't think – '

'What?'

She stood for a moment. Her eyes filled, suddenly, with tears.

'It's all right. It doesn't matter.' She brushed past him to the gate. 'Let's just go!'

10

'Do we know the way?' said Fran.

'Yes.' He had looked it up in the A-Z. 'Straight through to Brixton, then – '

'I'm not going to Brixton!' Harriet shrilled it out, in the silence of the road. 'There are black people in Brixton!'

Fran's face grew crimson. Shahid said, 'What's the matter with black people?'

'They'll beat us up!'

'Oh,' said Shahid. 'Really?'

Fran, looking uncomfortable, said, 'Don't be silly, Harry! That was race riots, years ago.'

'I don't care! I don't like it. I'm not going there.'

'Well, I don't know how else you're going to get to Barnet,' said Shahid, 'because that's the way I'm going.'

'I don't want to go to Barnet!'

'Oh, now, Harry, we've had all this out! We agreed . . . we're going with Shahid to his brother's.'

'I don't want to go to his brother's! I don't – '

'Ignore it,' said Shahid. 'Just walk on.'

He strode off, ahead of them. He felt like his father, striding ahead of his mother and sisters, except that his father had always been supremely and unquestioningly confident that his mother and sisters would be following him. Shahid was far from confident about Fran and Harriet; in fact he had to restrain a nervous impulse to look back and check. He tensed himself, waiting for Fran's voice to call after him, 'Shahid, we're going back!' He wasn't sure, any more, whether he would have the will to go on by himself. It wouldn't have bothered him before, but it did now.

He heard the swish of petticoats coming up behind him.

89

He turned. Harriet was weeping, piteously. Just for a moment his irritation melted. She looked so young and so vulnerable – and so ridiculously out of place in her absurd gear, like a little kid dressed up for a party which had never happened.

He stood waiting for them to catch up.

'You know that cycle shop in the High Street?' He addressed himself to Fran. It was as if he and she were parents, and Harriet their child. 'I thought we'd stop off and have a look, see if they've got anything.'

'You think they'll be open?'

She was almost as naïve as Rahim. He reminded himself again that Fran had been shut away in a Stone Age camp for the past four weeks.

'I don't think anything is going to be open,' he said. 'I think it's a question of just helping oneself.'

There wasn't much left in the cycle shop in the High Street: just one abandoned bike with a buckled front wheel. It seemed that people had been there before them, on a similar mission. It figured, thought Shahid. With no trains or buses, bicycles became the obvious form of transport for those such as himself who couldn't drive.

'But what do they want them for?' said Harriet. She said it somewhat fretfully. 'Where are they all going to? There's nowhere to go!'

'They're probably doing what we're doing, trying to get to relatives.'

'So where are they all? I haven't seen droves of people on bicycles. I haven't seen *any*one.'

It was true: thus far on their journey the streets had been deserted.

'I expect it's because they all set out weeks ago. Back at the beginning.' When perhaps they had still thought they had a chance of escaping, getting out while the going was good, cycling into the country with their saddle-bags and panniers full of food. It was a dream he had cherished, for just a short while, for himself and Roshana. Not that it would have worked. Roshana had been far too young. But tougher than this one, for all that. Roshana would at least have made an effort. She was a fighter. He looked rather sternly at Harriet. 'If I mended this bike for you, you could ride on it – if you changed out of those clothes.'

'The bike's broken.'

'Like I said ... I'll mend it!' He seized it, and set it upright. It looked as though people had had a fight, and trampled on it. A quick wrench and the buckled front wheel was more or less straightened out. 'There! One perfectly good bike.'

Capriciously, now that it was done, she said she didn't think she wanted to ride.

'Well, I'm still taking it!' Defiantly, he wheeled it out of the shop. One bike was better than no bike at all. 'We can ride even if you can't.'

They toiled on, down the main road, through the concrete deserts of West Croydon, of Thornton Heath, of Norbury. Now and again they would glimpse fugitive figures, masked like themselves, furtively busy about their own affairs. Nobody spoke. Nobody even acknowledged anyone else's presence. Shahid's hand, each time, would go to the back pocket of his jeans, tighten over the shaft of the knife, but nobody came close. There were troubles enough, without looking for them.

Abandoned cars littered the route, some probably still drivable if only he knew how. He thought for a moment of attempting it – after all, it couldn't be that difficult – but swiftly dropped the idea after approaching one and finding someone sitting in it. Harriet giggled and said, 'Fancy trying to steal someone's car when they're still inside it!' He wasn't sure whether she appreciated that the someone inside it had been dead.

They saw only one car actually on the road, and that was a white Rolls-Royce with a personalised number plate, well known in the district as belonging to a local builder. They heard it coming when it was some way off. It wasn't so much the unaccustomed sound of a car engine which alerted them as the loud blaring of music. It sounded like an

91

approaching carnival. The car was full of kids, at least a dozen of them, all leaning out of the windows waving rattles and shouting. It was driven by a black youth wearing a green hat with a feather in it. Some of the others had paper party hats. One was blowing a toy trumpet, another releasing yards of coloured streamers. Harry stood waving, blowing kisses as the car went past. One of the boys blew a kiss back at her.

'Are you crazy?' Shahid turned in a fury and slapped her hand down. He didn't slap it hard, but she gave a small cry of anger and cradled it.

'What did you do that for?'

'I said, are you crazy?' A load of kids could be trouble. The last thing he wanted was for them to stop and come back.

'We'd better get out of here.' He pushed at her. 'Go on! Quick!'

'Why?' She stumbled, deliberately, and dug her heels in. 'What do we want to go down there for?'

'Because I say so!' Fran, patiently waiting a few metres ahead with the bike, had already got the message. She turned and cycled down the road which he had indicated. He gave Harriet another shove. Grumbling, she allowed herself to be manhandled round the corner.

'I suppose you're just jealous!'

'Yeah, that's right,' said Shahid. 'I'm jealous.'

'Miserable old goat!'

The streets dragged on, dreary and deserted, interminable in their suburban sameness beneath the naked sun. Fran and Shahid took turns at riding the bicycle. They rode slowly, stopping to wait when they got too far ahead. Harriet drooped, complaining of the heat. Nobody said anything. She knew what the solution was.

They reached Streatham Common and stopped for a break and a can of fruit salad. They opened the fruit salad mainly for the liquid. Fran's mother hadn't gone in for tinned fruit juice or bottled water. He realised, too late, that they should have boiled some water and brought it with them. Just one of the (probably many) things they hadn't thought of.

'OK!' He snapped his fingers. 'Let's move it!'

Fran obeyed readily enough. Harriet, her small face screwed up in protest, had to be coaxed.

'Do you want to ride?' said Shahid.

She thought about it. 'Perhaps if I just took my hoop off – '

'No.' He shook his head. 'You'd get the skirt caught in the chain and louse the thing up.'

'I've got an idea!' Fran opened the carrier bag. 'Why don't you put your shorts on?'

'Shorts? Have you brought my shorts?' Already she was tearing at the buttons on the front of her dress. 'Why didn't you *tell* me?'

There wasn't anyone about, so it didn't really matter that she stood stark naked, save for a brief pair of pants, on the edge of Streatham Common. It just confirmed her general loopiness. Fran glanced across at Shahid and smiled, rather nervously. Shahid hunched his shoulders. Let her get on with it. Across the street, just for an instant, he thought he saw a face at an upstairs window. Someone enjoying a good perve, no doubt. Well, and why not? There wasn't much else to enjoy, these days.

Harriet, in T-shirt and shorts, jumped astride the bicycle and set off at a belt. (The precious dress, about which all the fuss had been made, was left in a heap, on the ground.) Fran called after her, anxious, like a mother hen: 'Harry! Don't go too far!'

'Oh, leave her,' said Shahid. At least this way they could get a move on.

Going over Vauxhall Bridge, approximately one hour later, they saw things like parcels floating in the water. Harriet, ahead of them – she was riding all the time, now – had stopped and was hanging over the parapet, staring.

'Look!' She pointed. 'What are those?'

'Bodies,' said Shahid.

Fran turned away. Harriet went on staring. 'What are they doing there?'

'They're dead.'

'But there are so many of them!'

'That's right,' he said. There were. He counted at least half a dozen.

'What are they doing in the water?'

How should he know what they were doing in the water? 'Maybe somebody threw them there.'

'Or maybe – ' she swivelled slowly to face him ' – maybe they threw themselves there.'

'Well – yes.' Maybe they did. It was disconcerting when she came out with these sort of remarks. You could never be sure, at any given moment, whether she was inhabiting her own private fantasy land – which she seemed to do most of the time – or whether she was on one of her flying visits to what passed for reality.

They pressed on, up the long, baking length of Vauxhall Bridge Road until they came to Victoria Station, where there appeared to be people camping out on the forecourt. For a moment it fooled even Shahid.

'There must be trains still running!'

His excitement was short-lived. As they drew closer it became apparent that the people in the forecourt, whatever it was they had been waiting for, had long since given up. He peered into the station, just in case, but it stood in silence, cavernous and empty. He had never seen a mainline station at a total standstill before. The sight, for some reason, chilled him far more than the sight of bodies in the forecourt. Perhaps because it really did seem to spell the end of the world.

He hastened out to the courtyard, where the two girls stood huddled together, waiting for him.

'Did you find anything?' said Harriet.

He shook his head. She giggled. 'That's a pity! I was looking forward to a day trip to Brighton.'

'Yeah. Just goes to show,' he said, 'doesn't it?'

'What's that?' She looked at him, inquiringly.

'A person could die waiting for British Rail.'

Harriet screeched. She found it funny even if Fran didn't. Fran's face, above her mask, looked white and drawn. He hoped she wasn't going to do anything silly, like pass out on him.

'It's what's known as sick humour,' he said.

'Oh, Fran hasn't got any sense of humour of any kind . . . she always sees the serious side of things.'

The remark struck him as exquisitely humorous in itself. Armageddon was upon them, and Fran could only see the serious side of things . . . how Simon would have loved it!

'Did I make a joke?' said Harriet.

That creased him even more. He and Harriet giggled together. After a bit, in reproachful tones, Fran said: 'Shouldn't we be moving? If we want to get somewhere by tonight.'

'Yeah.' He wiped his eyes on the back of his hand. 'Sorry. I know it's not really funny, but – ' Paroxysms gripped him yet again. Fran stood patiently waiting.

'Sorry,' he said. 'Sorry. You're quite right. Yes.'

'So which way do we go?'

'Ah-mm – ' He pulled himself together, making an effort to concentrate. He had never been a giggler. He supposed it came under the general heading of hysteria. 'Er . . . that way. I think.'

They walked in silence, watching Harry ride ahead on the bike. The road seemed longer than he remembered it from the A-Z, but it wasn't until Fran, in somewhat doubtful tones, said, 'Westminster Bridge?' that the realisation struck him: they had been walking in the wrong direction.

'Shouldn't we have gone more that way?' Fran waved a hand, westwards.

He agreed, bitterly, that they should.

He could have kicked himself. That was what came of making asinine jokes and not paying attention to where one was going. They must be at least a mile off course, and Harriet was looking decidedly the worse for wear.

'If we could just rest for a bit?' Fran suggested it timidly, obviously not wishing to upset him. (Was he really such an ogre? Shades of his father . . .)

'Don't worry,' he said. 'We'll find somewhere.'

They came to a park, which Fran agreed must be St James's. Other people had been there before them; tramps, he supposed. Or maybe not. Maybe just people like themselves who had stopped to break their journey and never moved on.

They selected a spot well away from the inhabited parts – he resisted the temptation to make a joke about choosing your neighbours – and settled down on the grass to eat a meal of cold baked beans and digestive biscuits, followed by a can of pears to quench their thirst.

Harriet tried saying she wasn't hungry. Shahid listened for a few minutes to Fran trying to coax her – 'Just a spoonful, Harry . . . please!' – then stepped in.

'Eat it!'

'I'm not hungry, I don't – '

'I said, *eat it*! It's because of you we've had to stop – because you're so weak. What are you trying to do? Starve yourself? You already look like a walking skeleton. If you think that's attractive, then you're out of your tree. No one's going to get turned on by a bag of old bones!'

Her cheeks reddened, angrily. Fran, kneeling, said, 'Please, Harry . . . please try!'

Sullenly, she took the baked bean tin.

'I don't know how you're supposed to eat wearing these stupid things!' She wrenched off the mask and threw it pettishly to the ground. 'I'm not wearing it any more, it looks ridiculous!'

'It'll look even more ridiculous,' said Shahid, 'if you come out in black blotches.'

'So what if I do? Who cares?'

He shrugged.

'Anyway – ' she nibbled fretfully at a single baked bean – 'people still die whether they wear them or whether they don't, so what's the point?'

There very likely wasn't one. Probably, if the truth were known, it had been nothing but a sop to boost public morale and they were all walking round making fools of themselves for no reason. Still, he wasn't prepared to be quite as cavalier as Harriet.

'It must give *some* protection,' he said.

'Why? It's only a bit of old gauze. What good's a bit of old gauze?'

Fran, who had been sitting in silence, frowning and pressing the soles of her trainers together, suddenly hooked her hair back and in the tones of one who is determined at last to face facts, said: 'You know when you said earlier that this time they'd really done it?'

'Yes.'

'What did you mean?'

'What I said . . . they'd really done it.'

'You mean you don't think it's just a – an ordinary illness?'

'Do you?'

'I don't know.' She bent her head over her trainers. 'I don't know what to think. I don't know enough about it.'

'Nobody knows enough about it – except the ones who are responsible. And they're not giving anything away.'

'They said on the television – the Environment people – they said something about . . . germ warfare.'

'They would!' Harry sounded scornful.

'Is that what you think?' Fran ignored Harry. She looked across at Shahid. 'Do you think it's germ warfare?'

'We don't actually have germ warfare,' he said. 'Not on our side. On our side it's called research . . . for purely defensive purposes. Like the Bomb. That's all we ever had the Bomb for. To stop The Others. *We* wouldn't ever start anything. It's just that this time it looks as though we have.'

'Why us?' said Harriet. 'Why not them?'

'It could just as easily have been them. Criminal stupidity isn't confined to any one country.'

Harry looked at him, resentfully. Fran said: 'But you don't think it was deliberate? I mean . . . whatever happened . . . it was an accident?'

'Only in the sense that something obviously went wrong. That doesn't mean to say it wasn't totally predictable. We've

97

always known that something had to go wrong sooner or later. It's been hanging over us for decades. It's just been a question of everyone keeping their heads down and praying it wouldn't happen in their lifetime. So, we're the unlucky ones: we copped it. The only thing is we all thought it would be the Bomb or the ozone layer. We forgot the nasty little bacterial messes they were cooking up behind their closed doors. One of them was bound to get out one day.'

'You really think that's what happened?'

'Do you have any other suggestions?'

She was silent. Harriet said: 'Plague.'

'No plague ever spread this fast.'

'What about the Black Death?'

'Not even the Black Death.'

'But they are *calling* it a plague,' said Fran.

'Well, they're not likely to call it a monumental cock-up, are they?'

'Oh!' Harriet plonked down the baked bean tin. 'You're so sure of yourself! Always think you've got all the answers.'

'All I'm saying is that if you mess with deadly germs then sooner or later you're going to get a deadly accident . . . and we've got it!'

'Yes – in London!'

'All over, from the sound of things.'

'Yes, but it *started* in London.'

'So?'

'So who's going to carry deadly germs through the centre of one of their own cities?' Harriet brought it out with an air of triumph.

'Who? I'll tell you who! Your precious Government, that's who! They've been carting nuclear waste through the centres of cities for years!'

'Nuclear waste is different.'

'Oh? How?'

'It's all in containers.'

'So this stuff was probably all in containers!'

'What *stuff*? What *containers*?' Harriet screeched it at him venomously. 'You decide there's stuff and we all have to accept it!'

'Did you know,' he said, 'that there's an island off the north-west coast of Scotland that they contaminated with deadly anthrax germs over half a century ago? Did you know that it's *still* contaminated, even today? Did you know that the flasks they stored the anthrax in were transported *six hundred miles*, all the way from the north of Scotland down to Wiltshire, in an *ordinary van*? What do you think would have happened if there'd been a crash? People like you would have been sitting around saying, "who's going to carry deadly germs through the centre of one of their own cities?"'

Harriet tossed her head. 'You're talking about fifty years ago! They don't do things like that now.'

'How do you know what they do and don't do?'

'Well, how do you?'

'I don't,' said Shahid. 'Nobody does. That's exactly how this sort of thing happens, because *nobody knows anything*. Small wonder we're all paranoid!'

'Speak for yourself,' said Harriet.

'All right! So what do you know of the things that go on? The things that are done in your name? In the name of *democracy*? What do you know about them?'

'As much as I need to know, thank you. That's what we elect governments for.'

'Right! You've said it ... that's what we elect governments for. To save ourselves the trouble of having to think. Well, we got what was coming to us! You duck out of all responsibility, you forfeit all right to scream when the balloon goes up ... we're like a load of kids! Silly little kids, playing in our playpens, while out there the psychopaths lay trails of dynamite and run around with lighted matches telling us it's all as safe as houses and all for our own good, and still we say, oh, we must have leaders! There's got to be someone in charge, someone to make the decisions, *we* can't do it! In any other circumstances that would be labelled immaturity. We sit here and call it democracy!'

'So what makes you think it's any better anywhere else?'

'I never said it was any better anywhere else!' This girl had a mind like a grasshopper. It was impossible to hold any sort of rational conversation with her. 'What's anywhere else got to do with it? Everywhere's just the same as here! One big nursery run by psychopaths!'

Harriet pursed her lips. 'It's all men's fault,' she said, 'anyway. It would never have happened if it had been left to women.'

'If it had been left to women we'd probably still be living in the Stone Age!'

Fran looked at him. 'That might not be such a bad thing,' she said.

It was early evening, already growing dusk, when they left St James's Park. They came out into a road which at first no one was able to identify.

'I thought you were supposed to know where we were going?' said Harriet. 'I thought it was all supposed to be straightforward?' It should have been. It had looked simple enough on the map. 'Haven't you ever been there before? He's your brother. Haven't you ever visited him?'

'Only a couple of times.'

'And you don't know which way you went?'

'We went by train.' Shahid and his mother and sisters. Rahim had met them at the other end. If he'd gone by car he would have remembered.

'Seems to me,' said Harriet, 'you're nothing but a mouth on a stick . . . all right at *talking*, not very much good when it comes to *doing*.'

It was Fran who rescued him. She said, 'I think this is the Mall. If we go that way – ' she pointed ' – we get to Trafalgar Square. Would that be all right?'

He seized on it, gratefully. He knew where he was with Trafalgar Square. It was still too far to the east, but he reckoned he could at least find his way from there.

He struck out, with renewed confidence. Everyone was entitled to the odd mistake.

'Admiralty Arch,' said Fran.

He nodded. Of course. He knew Admiralty Arch. He knew

this area like the back of his hand. They would be all right now.

Harriet, cycling ahead of them, had come to a halt. She turned and waved. She seemed excited.

'What is it?' Fran and Shahid set off towards her at a run. 'What's happening?'

'Look!'

Harriet was straddling the bicycle, tips of her toes pressed into the ground, leaning forward over the handlebars. They followed the direction of her gaze: the whole of Trafalgar Square was lit up. It looked like one vast bonfire. Cars (he thought he recognised one as the white Rolls-Royce which had overtaken them earlier) had been turned on their sides and were burning fiercely, thick billows of blackness plummeting into the air, along with leaping pillars of raw flame, rocketing upwards through the smoke, turning the night sky orange. In and out of the red and yellow tongues which licked and flickered at the edges could be seen a frieze of silhouetted figures, hands linked, capering faun-like through the ashes. Faintly, over the roaring of the fires, came the sound of music.

Harriet stood staring, as one entranced. On her face was the delighted smile of a child observing wondrous happenings. Even so had Roshana smiled, on her first visit to the pantomime.

'Shahid – ' Fran plucked urgently at his sleeve. 'I don't like it!'

'No.' Neither did he. He jabbed at Harriet. 'Let's go!'

She shook her head, never taking her eyes off the dancing figures.

'*Harry!*' Fran jerked at the bicycle. Harriet flew round. He could see her mouth opening to scream a protest: he got to her just in time. It was doubtful if anyone would have heard her over the raging of the fires, but he was taking no chances. With Fran wheeling the bicycle, he half dragged, half carried, a struggling Harriet across the broad sweep of intersecting roads and into the safety of one of the side streets. She turned on him, the minute he set her down.

101

'What'd you do that for, you pig? It was a party! We could have gone! They were having fun!'

'Oh, Harry, don't be stupid!' snapped Fran. 'Just act your age!'

Shahid was almost as taken aback as Harriet.

'I'm sorry.' Fran thrust at her hair. 'But honestly – ' Her voice trembled slightly. 'There's a time and place for everything!'

He would have thought Harriet would have sulked, or flown into one of her tantrums. Instead, wistful, almost entreating, she said: 'They were *people* – having *fun*.'

'They'd have had fun with us if they'd've caught us,' said Shahid.

By nine o'clock they had reached the Edgware Road. Harriet was drooping again, but worse than that was the state of the sky: black and suddenly threatening, after weeks of drought. Fran glanced at Shahid anxiously as the first drops of rain started to fall. He avoided looking at her.

'It won't come to anything.' He was getting to Barnet by hook or by crook. A few drops of rain weren't going to stop him.

The drops grew heavier, splatting down like soup plates. Shahid had his anorak: the girls had only brought sweat-shirts. He shook his head, irritably.

'They didn't say anything about this on the weather forecast.'

'Have there been any forecasts?' Fran sounded surprised.

'It was a joke,' he said.

'Oh!' She smiled, rather tremulously. 'I'm sorry. I'm not very good at jokes.'

'Don't worry about it. Like you said, there's a time and place.'

'Harry's right, though.' She said it humbly. 'I don't always see what's funny about things.'

'So you're in good company. I don't expect anyone else does, just at this moment.'

They were forced, in the end, to take shelter, huddled in

the doorway of a small shop, glumly watching as the heavens opened and the rain poured down.

'It's going to storm,' said Harriet. She was the only one who wasn't glum. She seemed quite happy, standing in the doorway looking at the rain. 'I wonder what all those people are doing, in Trafalgar Square?'

'Getting wet,' said Shahid.

'I don't expect they care. You don't, when you're having fun.'

The rain was coming down in buckets, slashing into their doorway, soaking them even as they huddled there. Already the first rumblings of thunder were rolling round the sky. Lightning, within seconds, had gone streaking after it, splitting the darkness wide.

'It's right on top of us,' said Fran.

Harriet gave a wild shriek and dashed out into the road. Shahid swore, and went after her.

'Get back in, you idiot! You'll get soaked!'

'I like getting soaked!' She flung up her arms exultantly as another flash of lightning went snaking over the sky. 'We ought to be at the party!'

'She's off her rocker,' he said. Fran did not dispute it. She looked at him, white-faced.

'What are we going to do?'

She was scared. He hadn't expected it of Fran. She seemed so phlegmatic, so dependable.

He turned, and peered through the door of the shop, trying to see what lay within. The next flash of lightning showed a grubby interior, tables piled high with paperback books. Second-hand porn from the looks of it. But any porn in a storm, he thought.

He set the rucksack on the ground and undid the straps. Fran watched, without saying anything, as he pulled out a tin of luncheon meat and two sweat-shirts. She watched as he wrapped one of the sweat-shirts round the tin and the other round his fist.

'What *are* you doing?' said Harriet.

103

'Breaking and entering. What does it look like? Just get out of the way!'

'This boy is *ridiculous*,' said Harriet. 'I don't know why we ever came with him.' She clutched at Fran's arm. 'Let's leave him and go to the party!'

'Oh, Harry – ' Fran sounded at the end of her tether. 'Do please stop it . . . I can't take any more!'

11

'Shahid!'

The voice came to him, faintly, through layers of troubled sleep. It seemed to him that it was his mother, calling him for school. He moaned a protest, drawing his knees up protectively into his chest before she could adopt her usual ploy of sending Roshana in. Roshana used his bed as a trampoline, his body as some kind of vaulting horse. Any minute now and he would be forced into wakefulness by the sound of her early-morning shrieks and gurgles, and the slightly queasy feeling of the mattress being bounced.

'*Shahid!*'

The voice came again, more urgently. He moaned another protest, drawing his knees in tighter. Familiar waves of sea-sickness engulfed him, but there weren't any thumps or gurgles, and the mattress wasn't bouncing. In fact, he didn't seem to have any mattress.

His first coherent thought was that he must be on the floor at home; that he had done his old trick of falling asleep in front of the television. Then it came to him that the television had stopped working, and anyway the floor at home was carpeted. This one felt like bare boards.

Tentatively he opened an eye. Just one eye; just the merest crack. He found himself staring at brown linoleum, torn and scuffed, thick with layers of grease. He seemed to be lying with his head next to a cooker. But it wasn't his mother's cooker. It wasn't his mother's kitchen.

In a rush it came to him: he remembered . . .

'Shahid!' said the voice. 'Shahid!'

He remembered heaving the tin of luncheon meat through

105

the glass and removing the broken shards with the sweat-shirt wrapped about his hand; clambering in ahead of the two girls and groping unsuccessfully for a light switch; waiting for the next streak of lightning, forking across the sky, to point him in the right direction.

At the back of the shop they had found a small room. The room where he was now: the room with the brown linoleum. He remembered Harriet worrying lest someone with a gun should come and shoot at them through the glass panels of the back door; or someone without a gun come bursting in through the front of the shop and throttle them. Nobody had laughed at the notion. To keep her happy – to keep them *all* happy – he had barricaded the back door with an upturned table and hooked a chair beneath the handle of the other.

It had been too hot for the sleeping-bag. Harriet and Fran had shared the blanket, using the sleeping-bag as a pillow, leaving Shahid to spread out his anorak. (It was the anorak he was lying on now.)

The storm had raged well into the night. They had switched off the light for fear of attracting attention and had lain there, in the darkness, listening to the thunder as it rolled overhead, and the steady drumming of rain on the roof, hearing it stream in torrents out of the guttering, swirling and sploshing in the yard outside. Every now and again a flash of white light had torn across the room, illuminating the girls on their blanket, Shahid on his anorak.

'Like *Macbeth*,' Fran had said. 'Like the witches . . . d'you remember, Harry, that time you played one of them?'

Harriet had said yes, she remembered. Her and Wendy Saintsbury and Julie Onslow.

'Julie reckoned old Dainty only picked on us 'cos she wanted us to look ugly.'

He had had no memory of Julie playing a witch. He did just vaguely remember Harriet. (Though nothing could ever have made her look ugly.)

'And d'you remember,' had said Fran, 'when we were little

106

'. . . when we used to stay with each other and we used to hide under the blankets and pretend it was the north pole?'

Harriet had said yes, they were being Arctic explorers.

'And we had to take care not to let any particle of air get in or we'd have got frostbite and had to have our limbs amputated.'

'And we used to lie there *suffocating* till it became so hot we couldn't breathe, hardly.'

'Didn't one of you ever fart?' Shahid had asked. That's what he and Simon would have done. That would have been the fun of it: gassing each other out.

There had been a silence, then Fran had said: 'Girls don't really go in for that sort of thing.'

She hadn't said it censoriously, nor even self-righteously, but still it had had the effect of making him feel coarse, and lewdly masculine. Anxious to join in (and to show them that he hadn't done only dirty *boy* sort of things) he had said, 'What about submarines? Under the bath water? Did you ever do that? You had to take the plug out and hold your breath and see if you could go without breathing until all the water had gone.'

They had said no, they had never done that. They had never done it and they hadn't seemed particularly interested in his having done it. They hadn't really cared about anything he had done. All they had wanted was to reminisce about what they had done.

Their exclusion had hurt him. Here it was, the end of the known world, and they wouldn't even talk to him. And yet at the same time as it had hurt him, it had seemed that it was not unjustified; that he had deserved to be excluded. He desperately hadn't wanted to be, but it had been only right that he should be. They hadn't known that, because he hadn't told them, but he had known it. He had known. He had known . . . what? What was it he had known? Something he hadn't told them . . . something bad. Something that had happened before they settled down, before the two girls had started talking. He had done something. Said something? Something he had kept from them. Something –

'Shahid!' The voice was talking at him again. It seemed to be pleading with him. It sounded frightened.

With difficulty, he forced swollen eyelids back over his eyes. He saw Fran, kneeling by his side.

'Shahid,' she said, 'are you all right?'

He struggled, unsuccessfully, to sit up.

'What is it?' whispered Fran. 'What's wrong?'

He opened his mouth to speak and felt a sickening lurch from the pit of his stomach. Before he could stop it, a stream of stinking vomit came spewing from his mouth.

He had just time to witness the horror in Fran's eyes before merciful darkness closed over him.

'There's nothing you can do,' said Harry. 'Even if you were a doctor. There still wouldn't be anything.'

'I know.' Fran thrust her hair back. Her fingers, as they hooked behind her ears, were trembling. 'I know there isn't.'

'So why hang around?'

'We can't just leave him!'

'Why not?'

'*Harry!*'

'I don't see what you're looking so shocked for. You've just agreed there's nothing you can do.'

'I can at least be here.'

'What for?'

'Well, in case he wakes up, or – '

'What?'

'I don't know!' Fran hooked again at her hair. 'Feels frightened. By himself.'

'Well, he won't. He won't wake up because people don't, they just die. And it could go on for *ages*.'

Fran thought of Mum and Dad, lying together on the bed. She thought of Harry's mum. She remembered thinking that if she had been Harry she would never have let her mother sink to such untended depths of squalor. She had wondered once or twice whether perhaps she had been unfair to Harry. After all, it had been Auntie Ellen who had made her promise to keep away (just as Fran's mum had

tried to keep Fran away, 'Darling, it is not a nice sight.')
Maybe it would have been more upsetting for her to have
had Harry there at her side than not to have had her. One
had to consider these things. But Shahid hadn't made
anyone promise. He hadn't had time.

'You'll go and get it yourself,' said Harry. 'You know that,
don't you? You're bound to. Everyone does. That's how he
got it. Hanging around, waiting for his father.' Shahid had
told them how he had waited for his father to die. Over a
week, he had said. It was usually only two or three days.
That was how it had been with the rest of them. His
grandmother. His mother. His sisters. Fran swallowed. 'It's
why we *haven't* got it,' said Harry. 'So far. But if you're
going to stay here and mess around with him . . . it's foul
and disgusting. And it *stinks*.'

Fran found herself trembling again. She pushed at her
hair. 'He can't help it.'

'But there's nothing you can *do*! There isn't any *point*.
You'll just get it yourself, that's all.'

Be happy, Mum had said. But how could she be, if she
walked out and left him? Surely Mum would understand?

'Why don't we go back to Croydon?' urged Harry. 'Back to
your place.' Cunningly, she added: 'There's food in your
place . . . stacks of it!'

'Afterwards,' said Fran. 'We can go back afterwards.'

'It'll be too late afterwards! There won't be any afterwards! You don't seem to realise . . . this thing is *catching*.'

'So maybe we've already got it.' They had been with
Shahid for twenty-four hours. They had slept with him in
the same small room. It was probably already too late. 'We
might just as well stay and die here as anywhere else.'

Harry made an exasperated noise. She jumped crossly to
her feet. (They had been sitting on the shop doorstep,
sharing a tin of grapefruit.)

'Of course,' she said, 'you never *were* a survivor . . . *I* was.'

She was referring to a time in class when Mrs Dainty had
asked them all to write down on a sheet of paper what they
would rescue if the house were on fire, 'assuming that all

your family and pets had been got out.' Fran had written, 'My mum's piano.' (She had only been twelve at the time.) Everyone had screamed with laughter. She hadn't immediately been able to see what was funny about it – her mum's piano had come to them from her great-gran. It wasn't specially valuable, but to Mum it was precious, even though no one could play it very well – but then Harry had scoffed, 'Like to see you trying to move that!' and of course she had seen at once how silly it was. Mrs Dainty, kindly, had said that Fran obviously had a self-sacrificing nature.

'Which comes rather low down, I'm afraid, on the list of qualities needed for survival.'

On her piece of paper Harry had written the one word, 'Nothing.' She was the only one who had. Fran couldn't remember what Shahid had written.

She picked up the empty grapefruit tin and walked back with it into the shop. There was a metal waste-basket behind the counter. Carefully, not to disturb Shahid in the room beyond, she placed the tin inside it. Harry stared, as if she had caught Fran in the act of doing something more than averagely lunatic.

'You're unbelievable,' she said.

Fran flushed. 'I can't help it. It's force of habit.' Mum had always kept the house so neat, it had become second nature to put things away where they belonged. She supposed, to Harry, it must seem ridiculous. Perhaps it was so. Bodies lying around unburied, and goody-goody Latimer meticulously placing empty tins into waste-baskets. But I can't help the way I'm made! she thought.

It was the way she was made which sometimes pushed Fran into doing things which she most desperately didn't want to do; like, for instance, opening the door which led into the back room and checking on Shahid. Checking that he hadn't been sick again. And if he had, then cleaning him up. Because what else *could* you do? No matter what Harry said . . . you couldn't just leave someone.

It had been appalling, this morning. She had thought she was going to be sick herself. Harry had screamed and fled.

The only thing which had kept Fran from doing likewise had been the thought, 'How terrible, if he realised.' She was almost certain that he wasn't in a state to realise – as Harry said, in self-defence, afterwards, '*He* doesn't know what's happening' – but those were the sort of thoughts which Fran had, and which led her to do the sort of things that Harry always used to grumble about and accuse her of making a martyr of herself over. (She knew that it was irritating. Someone, once, really *had* called her Goody-goody Latimer.)

She stood now, nerving herself to open the door. Harry, over on the far side of the shop, brooding amongst the books, had her lower lip stuck out in a familiar pout. Anything that had to be done was going to have to be done without Harry's help. Harry had never been good in emergencies.

Taking a breath, Fran eased the door just sufficiently to see in at an angle, to where Shahid was lying. He hadn't been sick again. But he was obviously uncomfortable, tossing and moaning on the blanket. He needed water; she should have thought of it before. She would have to boil some. She could make tea for her and Harry and keep the rest for Shahid.

In order to reach the cooker, she had to step across him. (She didn't like doing it, but he was too heavy for her to move by herself.) The cooker did not inspire confidence. It was an old, tinny-looking thing, with only two burners and a primitive oven the size of a shoe box. It reminded Fran of a toy stove she had once had when she was young. She wasn't even sure that it worked, but she flipped the switch which said COOKER and set the kettle on the front burner and waited, hopefully, for signs of something happening.

It took a long time, but it boiled in the end. She made the tea with some tea bags and powdered milk which she had found on a shelf, stood a jug to one side to cool, and proudly took the teapot and two mugs through to the shop.

'Look,' she said. 'I've made some tea.'

Harry turned. She was perched on the edge of the counter with the telephone in her hand. '*Tea?*'

111

'Yes.' Fran said it defensively. She didn't see what was so odd about making a cup of tea.

Harry screeched. 'Honestly, you're priceless!' She put on her comic charlady voice. 'I remember the day the world came to an end, I remember my friend Fran, she said, "I'll put the kettle on, and we'll all have a nice cup of tea."'

'You don't have to have any if you don't want.'

'No! I don't! I wouldn't touch it with a barge pole. Someone's manky old tea bags . . . they could have been there for years. And anyway – ' She jerked her head, distastefully, towards the door. 'It's hardly very hygienic,' she said, 'is it?'

Fran was silent. She looked down at her mug.

'I mean really,' said Harry. 'It hardly is, is it?'

She supposed it wasn't. But they couldn't live without eating and drinking, and she couldn't move Shahid out of the kitchen without someone to help her. She said so, in an apologetic whisper. Harry shouted, 'What are you whispering for? He can't hear you!'

That wasn't necessarily true. She remembered reading somewhere that people who had every outward appearance of being unconscious were sometimes able to hear everything that was said to them, it was just that they weren't able to respond.

'Oh, shut the door, can't you!' said Harry.

Fran pushed at it, with the tip of her trainer. (Anything to stop Harry being so disagreeable. She was a terribly up-and-down sort of person. Mercurial, some people had called it. Fran's mum hadn't. She had called it something quite different. Moody, was what Mum had called it.)

'What are you doing with the telephone?' she said. She was surprised to see Harry with it in her hand. Shahid had used it last night, to call his brother in Barnet and let him know they were on their way. Harry must have forgotten, or maybe she hadn't realised. Not that it mattered. Shahid had been wearing a mask, you couldn't spread germs through a mask, that was the whole point and purpose of them. 'Is it working?' she said.

'Yes, I'm ringing people. The trouble is I can't remember any numbers. Can you?'

Fran shook her head.

'Not *any*?'

'Only yours.'

'I'll ring that,' said Harry. She dialled, and sat listening. 'No one there. Shall I try yours?'

'No.' Fran said it sharply. She didn't like the thought of the telephone ringing and Mum and Dad lying there not able to answer it. She hooked her hair back. 'Try people out of the directory.'

'Which people?'

'Any people.'

'But it's the *London* directory . . . we don't know anyone.'

'Does it matter?' said Fran.

She left Harry working her way down the first page of the directory (L–R) and went back to look at Shahid. Her heart sank: he had been sick again. He was lying with his head in a pool of vomit. Fran felt her stomach rise into her throat. In panic she raced across the kitchen, out through the back door into the yard, lifted one corner of her mask and spat into a tissue. It was nothing; just ordinary bile. Trembling, she stood in the sunshine, gathering her courage to go back and face what had to be faced. Mum had faced it, with Dad. She hadn't just left him to rot. If Mum could face it, then so could Fran.

Under the sink that morning she had found a pair of rubber gloves. She put on the gloves and filled a bowl with water. Then she filled the sink and added bleach from a bottle which stood on the draining-board. With her gloved hands she moved Shahid's head out of the vomit and gently sponged him clean with a tea towel dipped in the bowl. She had already removed his mask earlier on. She had soaked it in bleach and hung it out in the yard to dry, along with his T-shirt. She had placed a T-shirt of her own beneath his head, so that if he were sick again the blanket would not be soiled. Now she took the second T-shirt and washed it in the water in the sink.

She hung the second T-shirt in the yard and pulled out the plug to let the dirty water drain away. From out of the carrier bag she took her spare pair of jeans and slid them beneath Shahid's head. It was essential the blanket should not be soiled. There was one patch on it which had been splashed. She poured out half a capful of bleach, filled the remainder with water, and dabbed at the patch with a corner of the tea towel. She knew that bleach rotted things, but she didn't know what else to do. On the television they had said to incinerate all infected material. That was all very well if you were in your own home. They hadn't said what to do if you were hiding in the back room of a shop in the Edgware Road with only a few spare knickers and T-shirts.

She washed out the tea towel by diluting the capful of bleach and hung it in the yard with the shirts. The water which she had boiled and left in the jug should be cool enough to drink by now. She took a plastic spoon from a drawer beneath the sink, washed it under the tap, took the spoon and the jug and went across to Shahid.

'Shahid?' she whispered. She raised his head from the sleeping-bag and trickled a few small drops of water into his mouth. He swallowed obediently, or maybe it was simply a reflex action. She knew that that was what it most probably was, for as Harry had said, he won't wake up, people don't, they just die, except that how could they know? There might be people, a few people, one or two people, who didn't. They didn't know everything.

'Shahid,' she whispered, 'please don't die . . .'

When she went back out to the shop Harry had grown tired of the telephone game – 'I've tried a column and a half and not one person's answered and half the time it doesn't even ring' – and was standing in the doorway, staring out at the street.

'Do you think there's anybody else alive in the whole of London?'

'There must be,' said Fran.

'Then why don't we see any of them?'

'I suppose because they're all staying indoors.'

'But what for? What are they waiting for? What do they think's going to happen?' Harry suddenly whirled round, almost knocking Fran off balance. 'I'm bored! I want to get out!'

'You were the one who wanted to stay put,' said Fran. 'You said you wanted us to shut ourselves up in your basement and wait for the Government to do something.'

'Government!' Harry's tone was scathing. 'What Government? There probably isn't any Government any more. They're probably all dead. Why don't we go to the party?'

'The party was last night. It won't still be on now.'

'It might be. Why don't we go and see?'

'Because it's not the right time for parties!'

'It is! It's *exactly* the right time for parties. Oh, you're such a fuddy-duddy! You're such a *bore*. You always were. I don't know how I've put up with you all these years. Whatever I suggest, you always find something wrong with it. Whenever I want to do anything, it's always the same, you're always such a wet blanket. D'you know what Wendy Saintsbury said to me once? She said, "I don't know why you go round with Fran Latimer, she's such a *drear*. She's so *boring*. I don't know what you see in her . . ." oh, Fran! I'm sorry! I didn't mean it!' Harry, in tears, launched herself at Fran. 'I'm sorry! I love you! I didn't mean it!'

They clung together, their arms wrapped tight.

'I don't know what I'd do without you,' sobbed Harry.

Half an hour later, she was nagging about the party again.

'Why won't you come? Just because of *him* . . . you didn't even like him when we were at school. You said he was arrogant. So what do you want to stay here now for, just because of him? What's it to you?'

'He didn't have to bring us,' said Fran. 'He could just have left us.'

'So why didn't he? We'd have been a lot better off! *I* didn't want to come. He didn't even ask us, he just *assumed* . . . I hate him! It's all his fault!'

115

At four o'clock in the afternoon, she suddenly exploded. 'I can't stay shut away like this! I'm going to go to the party even if you're not!'

She must have slipped out while Fran was tending to Shahid. Fran came back into the shop to find it empty, and the bicycle gone from where they had left it.

'Harry!' She ran outside and looked, but the Edgware Road was as empty as it had ever been. 'Harry!' she called. And then again, *'Harry!'* Her voice hung in the stillness. 'Harry,' she whispered. 'Oh, Harry, how could you?'

12

This is the journal of me, Frances Latimer. I am starting it on Day 1 of the Plague Year. Day 1 because this is the day on which I have decided to keep a record of what is happening. Plague Year because that is how I think of it. If there is anyone who would like to know who I am and what happened to me before this date they can find out from the diary which I kept when I was at home. Home was number 10 Raglan Court, South Croydon, in Surrey, and the diary was in the cupboard by the side of my bed. It says 'Private' on the cover, but whoever finds it has my full permission to read it. I think by then it will be an historic document.

I am at present residing, if that is the right word, in a second-hand bookshop halfway along the Edgware Road, in London. With me is Shahid Khan, who is a boy I was at school with. Shahid is suffering from the disease. He has been extremely ill, so that many times over the past week I have been scared that I will wake up and find him dead. It is terrible because there is so little one can do. Today he seems not quite as bad as he was yesterday. I am hoping and praying for him and keeping my fingers crossed, though I know that no one is supposed to be able to recover from this disease. But yesterday I truly thought it was going to be the end and today he is sleeping quite normally, or that is what it looks like, hardly any sweating at all, or being sick, which is the really worst and most awful part. However, I know that it may be only a temporary improvement so I am not letting my hopes run too high.

For a short time my best friend Harriet Somers was with us, but Harry left to go to the party. This was a party which was being held in Trafalgar Square and which I expect was well over by the time she got there. I have been waiting for her to come back, but she never has, and I have to accept that something has probably happened to her. I am trying not to think about it. There are lots of things I am trying not to think about; this is just one of them.

(On the other hand, Harry is so unpredictable that it is quite possible she found someone who said, 'I know where there is another party,' and she just went waltzing off with them. Harry is a bit like that. She has always been impulsive.)

The accommodation here comprises: one long dark narrow room filled with books (of the tatty variety), one small square room which is a kitchen, an outside lavatory and a minute back yard. It is not very savoury. The yard is full of rubbish, and the lavatory is disgusting. I have tried to clean it up but it has been difficult with Shahid so ill. He has been sick lots of times, and I have had to do things for him that I never would have thought that I could do, especially when it is someone I don't really know very well (in spite of us being at school together), but once you get used to it, it is not so terrible. Also, when there is no one but you then you just have to get on with it. Mum would understand though Dad would probably be horrified, he was always so embarrassed by anything like this. Naked bodies, things to do with sex. (Not that being ill has anything in itself to do with sex, but I mean Shahid being what Harry's mum used to call of the Opposite Persuasion.) Even after twenty years of being married Dad always used to get dressed and undressed with his back turned towards Mum. I never knew this until recently, when she told me in one of her confidential moods. (Mum and I had just started to do a lot of talking together. We were getting really close.)

The reasons I am writing this journal are several. They are as follows:

1. For posterity. If I survive and have children, then I

118

will keep it for them to read and hand down through the family. Mum would like this. If I don't survive then maybe other people will, and in generations to come they will read journals such as mine and know what it was like during this period. (I have decided that if Shahid gets better it will be A Sign: it will mean that we are both survivors. If he dies, then probably I will, too. Because if Shahid dies I don't think that I will be able to go on by myself. I know I promised Mum, but I am just not brave enough. That is another reason for keeping this journal. It is a sort of final testament.)

2. The second reason is that it gives me something to do and stops me dwelling on things – or at least if I do dwell, because sometimes you can't not, it helps me dwell positively instead of negatively. (It is positive when you feel that you are leaving something for the future.)

3. The third reason is that I think I should go mad if I didn't write it all down.

Harry went a bit mad towards the end. That is why she ran off to go to the party. There are moments when I can almost understand what made her do it – there is almost nothing worse than just sitting doing nothing – but it was mean of her to leave me. I know she couldn't help it, you can't help the things you do when the balance of your mind is disturbed, but sometimes just lately, when I've been thinking about her and thinking how she wasn't really herself any more, I've wondered whether that was quite true. Maybe she was always like that and I just never realised it. Or never let myself realise it.

Harry screamed at me before she left. She got so impatient with me, because she felt I was frustrating her. She told me that a girl at school had said she didn't know how she 'put up with me' all those years. Well, now I begin to wonder how either of us put up with the other, and whether we only put up with each other because we didn't have any choice. I'm not sure that anyone else could have put up with Harry. It's true that I was a bore and didn't mix with people and that no one would have wanted

119

me for a friend, but it is also true that Harry was selfish and demanding. Shahid was right when he accused her of being neurotic. But I still wish she hadn't gone off. It has been dreadful without her, with no one to talk to, and being scared all the time in case Shahid was going to die. (Which he still might. I mustn't let myself get too hopeful.)

I am sitting on the counter writing this and have the door into the kitchen propped open so I can keep an eye on him. He hasn't been sick for almost twelve hours now but he is not really properly conscious and even though I talk to him, pretending he can hear me, I am not at all sure that he can.

We have been here for just over a week. For the first two days after Harry left I was so petrified that I hardly dared come into the shop at all. (The window is broken where Shahid punched a tin through it, which means that anyone could easily get in.) Then we ran out of food – well, I ran out of food, because Shahid hasn't been eating, if he had been eating we would have run out a lot earlier – and I didn't have any choice. I not only came into the shop but actually set foot outside. It was very scary but now I am growing used to it, at least a bit. I have found some places quite nearby where you can pick things up. I suppose what I really mean is where you can steal things. After all, they do still belong to people even if the people are dead, only one can't afford to think like that if one is going to survive. Even Dad would understand that.

Anyway, the fact is I have become quite an expert at finding things. I am like a sort of human magpie. I have found loads of tinned stuff, and some sheets and towels, and yesterday I found some books which I brought back, because although we are living in a bookshop there is actually nothing here that one can enjoy reading. (I tried some the other day because I had nothing else to keep myself occupied and it is all violence and sex.)

There is also an old television set here, on a stool at the end of the counter. I have switched it on several times but either it is not working or there is just nothing being shown any more. Tomorrow I will see if I can find a radio. There are television sets in the places where I pillage but I am not yet bold enough to try them. I just take what I need and go.

Sometimes I see other people. Not very often to begin with, but more and more as the days go by. They are all obviously doing the same thing and they are almost always on their own. None of them looks at all threatening. They just look furtive and scared. I saw a man the other day carrying what looked like a crowbar (what I think is a crowbar) but even he didn't look violent. He was probably only carrying it to protect himself (like I carry Mum's kitchen knife, which I discovered Shahid had brought with us), or to break into places. There is also a girl I have seen once or twice. A bit older than me and very thin, as if she has been ill or hasn't eaten for a long time. I wish I could screw up the courage to speak to her. It seems so silly, everyone avoiding everyone. We are all just terrified, I suppose. But what is it that we are terrified of? Are we terrified of catching the disease or are we terrified of being knifed or strangled? I suppose it is mainly the latter; at least, it is with me. It's like in the old days when you didn't get into a railway compartment by yourself if there was a lone man in it, and you didn't walk down dark alleyways or across the allotments late at night. Just in case. I can't decide whether there is more or less reason for being cautious now. After all, there are so few of us left (at any rate, in London) that it would seem much more sensible if we all got together.

The other day I tried telephoning people. I rang a girl called Susie Jenkin-Wright, whom I met at a camp I went to in August (which now seems like months ago but in fact is only a few weeks). I couldn't remember her number so I looked it up in the directory. I spent ages finding it because I didn't know whether it would come under J or W (it came under J and there was only one in the whole of London). Activities like this are a godsend because they fill up the time. In the old days I would have been impatient, not knowing where to find someone's name. Now I do it very slowly and carefully and am happy when I find it has taken me ten minutes. I think, 'That is another ten minutes gone.' Mum used to say one shouldn't wish one's life away, but she could never have imagined anything like this.

Anyway, when I had found it I rang Susie's number but nobody answered. I tried lots of times without any result. I couldn't remember the surnames of other people I used to know who lived in London. Most of the people I knew lived in Croydon and there is no Surrey directory here – and needless to say there is no reply on directory inquiries. Not even a recorded message. Also, as Mum said, you can't ring anywhere outside the London area. I have tried Gran lots of times. I try her every day, but it is no use.

Yesterday I remembered the surname of someone else I was at camp with, a boy called Steven Prior. I remembered that he lived in north London. I rang about ten Priors in north London before anyone replied, and then it was so terrible I wished I hadn't. Someone picked up the receiver and I said 'Hallo?' and there was just silence, though you could tell that there was someone there, so then I said, 'I'm trying to get in touch with a boy called Steven Prior,' and still there was silence, so I said, 'Hallo? Is anyone there? Please say something!' and suddenly there was this tiny little child's voice, all faint and faraway, saying 'Mummy, Mummy, Mummy,' just over and over. I kept saying, 'Who are you? What is your name? Are you all by yourself?' and all it said was 'Mummy, Mummy, Mummy...' until in the end the line went dead. I couldn't bring myself to ring back and now I can't get it out of my mind. I have these awful pictures of some tiny little child on its own in a house with everyone dead. I keep waking in the night and torturing myself with it, so that now whenever I wake I have to start gabbling through the alphabet or counting up to a thousand very quickly before it gets a hold of me.

What makes it so awful is that I know it's not just me being morbid. I know that it's probably true, and that this child won't be the only child. I know there must be *dozens* of children terrified and on their own. Then I think of what Shahid said about the epidemic probably being the result of an accident, but one which could have been foreseen if we hadn't all been so ostrich-like and immature, and that just makes me feel even worse. If it's an act of God, or nature, it's somehow easier to bear. Of course Shahid could be wrong, but even if he is it doesn't alter the fact that we *were* all ostrich-like and immature. Dad used to say, 'It's our job to look at the issues and elect people. Once we've done that, that's our part over with. It's not up to us to run the country.' He specially used to say it when he saw demonstrations on the television, like people marching against nuclear dumps, or students fighting with the police. He used to say, 'We live in a democracy. There are proper channels for voicing protests.' I used to agree with him once, but I don't any more. I think that was just Dad's way of opting out. I wish he were here, so we could talk about it.

I almost wish that *anyone* were here, so I could just talk about *anything*. I know Harry used to accuse me of being anti-social (because of my not liking parties and shutting myself away painting), but it is a very dreadful and isolating experience not to have exchanged one single word with another human being for as long as I have. I do say things to Shahid, but that is not exchanging words as he can't say anything in return, and I am not even sure whether he can hear me, although I begin to think he might be able to. I said to him today, 'Please, Shahid, please keep fighting,' and I'm certain he squeezed my hand. That sounds very corny but it is true.

When I was shaking out his anorak this morning (I have been sleeping on it) something fell out of a pocket: it was a packet of contraceptives . . . I couldn't help wondering what they were doing there. Do boys carry them round with them all the time, or did he put them there

123

specially, just in case? Like emergency rations? Harry once said that a girl at school called Wendy Saintsbury carried them in her bag even though she was a virgin because she said that one day she might want to stop being a virgin and the boy she might want to stop being it with might not have any. I suppose it could have been true. Wendy Saintsbury had loads of boyfriends. I have never had a single one and now, probably, never will. Unless perhaps Shahid – but I won't think of that.

I've noticed that in films about holocausts and disasters and such it's always a young girl and an old man, right at the end, who have to get together for the sake of the future. I don't think I could do that, not with an old man, though maybe I could if it was all there was. I could do it with Shahid, but I expect most people could do it with Shahid. When he is not ill he is very good-looking. I am not at all the sort of girl he would normally go out with. But maybe now there is not so much choice – well, anyway. We shall see. I still think it's odd how in books it's always this young girl with an old man, never an old woman (though young enough to bear children, of course) and a young boy, which I personally think would be far more interesting.

Last night I had a dream that we were back in the old days, before the disease. The only difference was that there were no men. I don't know whether the men had all died or whether there had simply never been any, but the world was just women and children. The children were neither boy-children nor girl-children but something in between.

I have been trying to think what it could mean. (I don't believe that dreams tell what is to come, I think they are the things that are going on in our subconscious swimming to the surface while we are asleep.) Does it mean that I blame everything that has happened on men (like Harry did) and think the world would be a better place without them? This is the obvious interpretation, and perhaps there is some truth in it, but only some. I certainly don't think the world is a better place without my dad, and I certainly don't want Shahid to die and leave me on my own. And I don't even think it is all men's fault, what has happened. Some women are just as aggressive as some men, Margaret Thatcher was, for instance. But then there are men who are very non-aggressive and gentle, like my dad. But Dad opted out, and I think that is what too many women did. It is very difficult, when there are those people who want power over other people and will stop at nothing to get it: it is very difficult for all the people who don't want power, except just power over themselves, to find a way of resisting it. The only way is by force of numbers, not to let them get that power in the first place, because once they have got it, it is almost impossible to get it away from them, and besides, people get used to being bossed around and told what to do and think that without someone to take charge society would all go to pieces.

It keeps coming back to what Shahid said, about people growing up and learning to take responsibility.

I have discovered that writing is rather like talking: it is very difficult to start, but once you have actually got going it can also be very difficult to stop. The reason I don't want to stop is that I am scared of being on my own. At least when I'm writing this journal it's like conversing with someone. When there were hundreds of people all round me, such as at school, for instance, I never wanted to converse with them, I only wanted to shut myself away and paint. You would think I'd be happy now by myself but I hate it. Maybe I should try to find some drawing paper from somewhere.

This is a cash book that I'm writing in. I found it under the counter in the shop.

Now it is tomorrow, day two of the Plague Year, but the twelfth day that we have been here.

Shahid is really getting better! I am convinced of it. This morning he actually knew who I was and talked to me. The first time that he has done so. He is too weak to do anything for himself but he drank a cup of soya milk (I found *six litres* yesterday in a place round the corner) and the test will be if he can keep it down. It is now over twenty-four hours since he has been sick. I am letting myself be a little bit hopeful, though only a little bit. If anything were to happen now it would be even worse than it would have been before, when I had no hope at all.

Why am I always such a pessimist? It used to get Harry mad. She used to say that I was *dismal*. It is true, I do expect bad things rather than good, and even when they are good I worry about when they will stop being good. I suppose you could say that in this case events have justified me, except that even in the midst of all that has happened there is still one little bit of me that desperately wants to go on living and to be happy, partly for Mum's sake, because I promised her, but partly for my own, as well . . . I *do* want to grow up and see the future and have children and tell them of the old times; and if I didn't think there was any possibility of it then I might just as well go and do what Harry did.

Sometimes I have thought that Harry was actually far braver than I am, because after all it's surely better to go out with a bang than just hang on, which is what I am doing. When I get those moods I think to myself, really and truly what is there to hang on *for?* Even if Shahid gets better and we go to his brother in Barnet, what is the point? Life will never, ever be the same as it was. But then, in other moods I think that life is for living just as long as one can. I remind myself that there are still trees, and grass, and flowers. And Shahid . . .

I have decided. If Shahid dies, I shall go and look for Harry. But if he lives, then it means we are survivors.

Yesterday morning I went on a foraging expedition and found some pencils and a block of paper in a stationer's-and-tobacconist's in one of the side streets. (It had already been pillaged; most places have. *No* cigarettes, *no* edibles, *no* bottles of pop, but all the paper you could want.)

Anyway, I thought I would try to draw portraits of Mum and Dad as I remembered them (oh, why didn't I bring photographs? I dread the thought that one day I might forget), but I couldn't do it. It made me cry too much and I had to stop. So then I thought I'd do a landscape – well, seascape, actually – the beach near Gran, down in Cornwall, but that made me cry even more, remembering all the holidays we'd had there. Everybody so happy, never dreaming what was to come. In the end I didn't draw anything but just felt wretched so decided to write my journal instead.

It's strange, the layers of misery that there are. You get used to feeling pretty miserable most of the time – what might be called 'low-level misery' – a sort of permanent *background* of misery, and you learn to cope with it, it almost gets to feel normal. But then something happens, like me trying to draw something, which reminds you of what it was like *not* to feel miserable, and it hurts so much you almost just can't bear it.

While I was out I saw the thin girl again. She was carrying a plastic bag full of something heavy (tins, probably) and when she saw me she sort of twitched one corner of her mask and I did the same – actually I smiled, and maybe she did, it's hard to tell. But if I see her again I shall definitely say something.

Afternoon. Shahid has drunk some more soya milk. It is really good that I was able to find soya milk as it is much easier to digest than cows'. We had soya milk at the camp I went to. The reason we had it there was not a health reason but because it was a vegan camp and vegans don't believe in dragging calves away from their mothers and slaughtering them so that human beings can drink their milk. I am in agreement with this.

I was going to talk to Mum about becoming a vegan, but now in *extremis* I am eating and drinking whatever I can find. But basing a whole philosophy of life on what you would do in *extremis* does not seem to me to be right. Like in the First World War when they would ask people who didn't want to fight, 'What would you do if a German soldier tried to rape your sister?' and if they said, 'I would use physical force if necessary,' they'd say that proved you weren't really a pacifist. It didn't prove anything of the sort! If we all based our philosophies on what we'd do in the worst case, then why not, for instance, eat human beings? After all, that's what people have done in plane crashes when human flesh was all there was.

I have just broken off to try telephoning Gran again. I knew I wouldn't be able to get through but now I can't even get any dialling tone. It looks as though the telephone has gone. And I was going to ask Shahid if he would like me to ring his brother for him. I would have done so before only I don't know his number and there are two whole pages of Khans in the directory. The last time he heard from Shahid was the very first night that we were here, and he was expecting us to arrive in Barnet the next day. He must be worried out of his mind.

It has only just struck me: why didn't I go through all the columns of Khans until I found one that lived in Barnet? I didn't think of it, that is why.

Evening. I have just looked in the telephone book and I don't think that it covers Barnet. Although Barnet is in the area that is cordoned off it is not actually part of London. So I couldn't have telephoned Shahid's brother anyway. That has made me feel a little bit less guilty.

This is the third day. Shahid is better even than he was yesterday. He managed to sit up by himself and eat some cereal for breakfast. (The cereal is repulsive and stale but I suppose it still has some goodness in it.) He said to me, 'How long have I been sick?' and when I told him I could see he didn't believe me. He said to me a bit later, 'Are you sure I've been sick so long?' And then, when I finally managed to convince him, 'Was I *really* sick?' I knew that what he was trying to discover was whether it was the disease or just an ordinary bug. I said, 'Yes, you were very sick,' and hoped he would leave it at that but still he persisted. He said, 'What sort of sick?' and I knew I would have to tell him in detail. He listened without saying anything, so in the end I said, 'Was that how it was with your father?' and he said, 'Yes – except that he died,' and we sat staring at each other for a long time, not really able to believe it. *Everybody* dies of this disease. There isn't any known cure. They said so, on the television. (At least, that is what Harry told me.)

Shahid and I had a long discussion about what it could mean. Did it mean that they were wrong (they often are wrong) and that it is possible for certain people to recover? Certain people, in certain circumstances? Shahid told me about a cut he had had on one of his fingers. He tried to show me, but I couldn't really see anything. We speculated whether perhaps it had acted like an inoculation and that he had had the disease but only in a mild form (except that it didn't seem to me there was anything very mild about it, it was still hideous).

I told him about the people I was starting to see on my foraging expeditions, and we wondered whether these were people who had had the disease and recovered or people who had never had it at all; and whether there were some people who had some kind of natural immunity or whether it was that they had just been lucky (so far).

We talked about the different ways you could catch it, and Shahid asked me what I had had to do for him (he didn't like some of the things I had had to do, you could tell, he looked really embarrassed), and said he hoped to goodness I hadn't run any risks. I said no, I had used rubber gloves all the time and had worn a mask, and we discussed whether he would need to wear one now that he had had the disease and recovered from it or whether it was like mumps and once you'd had it you couldn't get it again. I said it was always better to be safe than sorry and that in a chemist's shop nearby (where I had gone to look for Tampax, only I didn't tell him this) I had discovered a whole boxful of masks, still in their foil containers. Most of the stuff from the chemist's shop had been taken, all the medical things and anything that was eatable or drinkable, and I suppose the drugs, but nobody had taken the Tampax *or* the masks. I took two boxes of Tampax and ten masks. At first I thought that perhaps I had been greedy taking so many – so many masks that is – and then thought that maybe I hadn't taken enough, because who knows how long we shall have to go on wearing them?

I said to Shahid, 'Do you think we'll have to wear them from now until the end of our lives? Or do you think it's something that will burn itself out?' Shahid said he didn't know. He told me about his friend Simon's theory about the virus (if it is a virus) being airborne, which would mean that it might clear from certain areas and go into others; but unless you were an expert in wind and weather patterns you would never know where it was going to be, or whether any of it had got left behind. Also, it might or might not be the sort of thing that loses its potency. It could be like nuclear waste and still be around in thousands of years.

We both agreed that we didn't have enough knowledge even to make any intelligent guesses. It comes back to the same old thing: we don't *know*.

'We don't know anything,' Shahid said, 'because they never tell us.'

It's possible, I suppose, that they don't know themselves – assuming that there are any 'they' left, even – but he's quite right, even if they did know they wouldn't necessarily tell us. Or they might tell us just a little bit, to keep us quiet. Shahid reminded me that years ago there had been a terrible accident at one of the nuclear power stations, the one that is now called Sellafield but used to be something else (Windscale, or something). He said that at the time there was a real possibility that it might have turned into a Chernobyl-type disaster, maybe even worse, but the public was never told about it; not till decades later. They still went on telling us it was 'safe'.

'Like aluminium in the water,' I said. I could also have

said pesticides in the food chain or holes in the ozone layer or low-level radiation. All these things which those in power have dismissed as 'scaremongering'.

Shahid said, 'Precisely!' He said who knew what else had happened, and might still be happening, that we knew nothing about. I told him about how I had been thinking about what he had said before, in St James's Park, when he had argued with Harry, and how I was coming more and more to agree with him.

It was then that he suddenly said, 'Where *is* Harriet?' and I had to tell him she had gone. He said, 'And you didn't go with her? I hope it wasn't because of me?' I lied and said no, but I don't think he believed me. He said he felt guilty about it, because of Harry being my friend and it being all his fault for having dragged us with him. I tried to tell him it was all right, I said Harry wasn't herself and even if we'd stayed in Croydon she would probably still have snapped under the pressure (because Harry *couldn't* take pressure, she was never very stable, I realise that now) but I could see it didn't solace him. He kept brooding over it, and I got worried in case he had a relapse (I just couldn't bear it if anything should happen at this stage) so I didn't tell him about the telephone not working, which was what I had been going to do. I told him about the television instead, and asked him if he had any ideas on what might be wrong with it. People usually cheer up when you ask their expert opinion about something, and I remembered that at school Shahid had always been good at all those technical things, like maths and computers, that I couldn't cope with owing to my Stone Age mentality, and he did get a bit happier when I lugged the set in to him and dumped it by his side with a screwdriver which I found under the counter.

I left Shahid playing with the television while I went out foraging. (We don't actually need any more stuff at the moment, but I think I have inherited Mum's hoarding mentality and feel that one ought to accumulate what one can while it's still there. I suppose that is rather anti-social really, but it's insecurity that makes one behave like it. If one *knew* there would be enough then one wouldn't grab. That was another thing that was bad about the way we used to be. It was all grab grab grab while one could in case tomorrow one couldn't.)

I didn't see the thin girl today because I walked in a different direction from usual. But I did see a car! And two people on bicycles. I really begin to wonder if the worst that is going to happen – at least in this part of the country – has happened, or whether people are only emerging because of lack of food. I didn't find anything today, by the way. It was all houses, and while I expect there might be food in some of them I am not brave enough to risk breaking in. So far I have only gone into shops where other people have already been.

When I got back Shahid said he didn't think there was anything wrong with the television or with the plug, he said he thought there simply wasn't anything being transmitted. He said, 'You know what that means, don't you?' I said, "Yes, it's spread to the rest of the country," and I thought of Gran, down in Cornwall, and wondered if it had spread there. I also thought that if I had known about it spreading anyway, and about it probably being airborne, we could have gone down to Cornwall before, while we had the chance. I was scared at the time because I thought it was something that was confined to London and that it wouldn't be fair if people from London selfishly went and infected other people. I feel really annoyed with myself now. That is what comes of being goody-goody; I can see why Harry used to get mad at me. I don't suppose, if we went back to Croydon, that there would still be a way out. They must have blocked it off ages ago. The woman with the two children would have told someone about it.

We spent the afternoon reading, and in the evening we talked. I told Shahid about wanting to go to art school, and how futile and unimportant it now seemed. He said it wasn't in the least unimportant, nothing that made a person happy and fulfilled could possibly be regarded as unimportant, but all the same he was glad that he had never had any special ambition because it meant it was easier for him, now, to face the fact that life was never going to be as it had been. He said in many ways he thought that that was just as well, and maybe the few of us who are left will learn to grow up and take responsibility for our lives instead of handing it over to others.

What he says makes sense, especially when he says it just ordinarily, like this, in conversation, and not ranting or lecturing. Not that Shahid ever did either of those things, in fact I never knew before now what his views were, but his friend Simon used to. Shahid said that was because Simon was the sort who, although well meaning and rightfully angry, would probably have ended up as a career politician and become part of the very system he was trying to do away with.

We discussed whether there really *will* be only a few of us left – a few of course meaning thousands rather than just a handful. Thousands sounds like a lot when at the moment there are just him and me, but of course compared to the billions that there were it is nothing. I wondered if it was possible, Britain being an island, that this would be the only country affected; but Shahid seemed to think this was just wishful thinking on my part. He said if it's airborne there is no way the rest of the world can have been spared; and if it isn't airborne then it is difficult to see how it can have spread so quickly. We agreed that the rest of the world probably won't have escaped and that if the virus (?) remains as lethal as it has been then there is not very much hope for humanity. But maybe it will lose its force after a time. We just don't know.

The fourth day. Now that he is definitely getting better Shahid is becoming *masterful* (bossy, in other words). I told him this morning about the telephone not working and asked him if he would like me to try one of the public ones and ring his brother for him. He at once said no, it was too risky (why???) and that while he was on the subject I was not to go out foraging any more. I might have retorted, who is he to lay down the law? I have been managing very well all this time on my own. I didn't, because it is such a relief that he is better, and also a relief to have someone to talk to and to share the burdens.

Shahid said that he had been looking round at all the stuff I have collected and he really couldn't think there was anything else we could possibly need, but that if there was then he would be the one to go. Since, at the moment, he is still too weak to do more than walk to the lavatory and back (it is not so disgusting now as I have scrubbed it with bleach) I really can't imagine how he thinks he could go foraging. But I didn't want to puncture his masculine ego any more than it has already been punctured by having to have me do all these mortifying things for him ('things of an intimate nature,' as Mum would have called them). So I explained to him about my having a hoarding mentality, and agreed that since we shall presumably be moving on as soon as he is fit enough I couldn't see that we should have much need for anything else. But I said that when we moved on we ought to fill the rucksack, and even get another if we can find one, because you just never know what is going to happen.

I hadn't intended it as a criticism, but he immediately took it that way and said again that it was all his fault, us being stuck here, and Harry going off, and me having to forage for food. He reminded me that if I had had my way I would have filled the rucksack from the word go, it was him who said no. I pointed out that if he hadn't got ill we would have been in Barnet over a week ago, so in principle he had been quite right, but he said that was not so, in principle I had been right, wanting to provide for all eventualities.

I am sure in the old days he wouldn't have felt guilty and said it was his fault. When we were at school he always seemed so sure of himself. So *arrogant*. I wonder now if he really was like that or if it was just the way he came across. Like I came across as goody-goody, but really I am *not*. For instance, I teased Shahid today about the things that fell out of his pocket, and he got quite embarrassed. I think he actually blushed, though it's quite hard to tell when someone is dark. But he was definitely ashamed! I think part of the reason he was ashamed was that it was *me*. If it had been someone like Wendy Saintsbury, or Julie Onslow, or even Harry, he would probably have made one of those awful 'come on' sort of jokes that boys make, but nobody expects goody-goody Latimer to know about such things. (And it is true, if I had picked up his anorak, say, last term and contraceptives had fallen out of the pocket I would have blushed bright scarlet and wouldn't have said a thing. I would have pretended not to have seen. I have become far more liberated now, which is sad when I consider that it has all happened too late. I keep thinking what a lot I missed out on through being so introverted. I am not referring to *sex* but all the other things. Being sociable, I suppose.)

The fifth day. Shahid is now eating properly. That is a great relief because I have been scared that the disease, even if by some miracle a person did recover from it, might have terrible lasting effects, and of course it still might, it is the old thing, we *don't know*, but at least for the moment he is almost back to normal, just very weak still.

Today we discussed going to Barnet and Shahid complained that it was starting to sound like a line out of 'that dreadful play' we did last term. I asked him indignantly what dreadful play he was talking about, and he said, 'The Three Old Girls or whatever it was.' I said coldly (because I knew perfectly well that he knew), 'You mean *The Three Sisters*, and it isn't a dreadful play, it's one of my favourites of Chekov.' Shahid said Chekov was a bore and we argued about it for a bit, and then he said, 'Well, anyway, it sounds like that line they kept on about, *we must go to Moscow...*all I ever hear you say is, *we must go to Barnet.*' I said, 'Well, it's your brother, and he'll be out of his mind with worry by now.' 'Oh,' said Shahid, 'he's probably given me up for dead, I don't expect he'll care . . . one less mouth for him to feed.'

He explained how his brother was a devout Muslim and went to the Mosque and kept all the holy days, Ramadan (?) and everything, and looked upon Shahid as an infidel – 'Decadent and Westernised.' I pointed out that they were still brothers and that I thought Shahid ought to telephone him. He has promised to do so as soon as he is strong enough to get to a telephone. The nearest one is about five minutes away.

The sixth day. As well as having a hoarding mentality I have a horrible feeling that I have a nest mentality. This dreadful place is almost starting to seem comfortable. When we barricade both the doors at night and light one of the candles which I found under the sink (just as well, for we have no electricity any more: it gave out yesterday) and settle down with our mugs of soya milk, I am filled with thoughts of how cosy it is. And yet in reality it is *grim*. The sink is stained and the walls covered in grease. We lie on blankets on the floor and because I am too scared to go outside to the lavatory in the dark and Shahid is still wobbly on his legs we use a bucket, in absolutely full view of each other, because a) there is nowhere we could put it to be private, and b) even if we did we would still hear each other sploshing, and c) I have now seen all that there is to see and I expect Shahid had seen it already and when you are living cheek by jowl in a ghastly pit there really doesn't seem to be very much point in false modesty. Or indeed in *any* modesty. It is far less embarrassing being open like this. (Only a few weeks ago I would have suffered agonies.) But the point is that this ghastly dreadful hole has actually come to seem (almost) acceptable, which I suppose either shows how infinitely adaptable the human being is or how readily we lower our standards.

I tried to discuss this with Shahid, but I had just told him that 'We're sitting here drinking our night-time drinks like some old married couple,' and I don't think he liked the idea too much because all he did was grunt and say, 'You can get used to anything, given time.'

I don't believe that I shall ever get used to Mum and Dad not being here.

The seventh day. Shahid went out this morning. I went with him, in case he came over faint, but he said he was all right, just a bit woozy. He went as far as the telephone box and it was vandalised. I wondered if the person who had vandalised it had done it *before* or *after*; and if he had done it before how he would feel now, knowing all that has occurred. Shahid said the sort of person who would vandalise telephone boxes wouldn't feel anything. His view of human nature is more jaundiced (I think that is the word) than mine.

While we were out I saw my thin girl. I had meant to talk to her; I wish I had. Instead, all I did was twitch at her again. She twitched back, and I am sure she *would* have talked. I said to Shahid, 'That's the girl I see all the time. We ought to go back and say something to her,' but he came over all butch and masterful and wouldn't let me. He couldn't actually hustle me physically because he's not strong enough yet, but he did verbally. I think it's what's called lambasting – or at any rate, lecturing. He said, 'What do you think this is, social get-together time? You'll be wanting her to drop by for a coffee next.' I said, 'Well, why not?' I told him that he was manifesting a classic siege mentality and that I didn't see why I shouldn't at least have said hallo. He said that hallo would lead to other things, such as getting friendly and trusting her and telling her where we were holed up. I said, 'So what's wrong with that? Maybe she could join us.' Shahid said that what was wrong with it was that for all we knew she could be part of a gang.

137

I thought about this. I thought that I hadn't actually *seen* any gangs, or even any evidence of gangs. I told him that I agreed the girl might be part of something, but that a) if she was there was no reason to suppose that they would be hostile, and b) why call it a gang? Why not just call it a group? and c) if we were going to view everyone with suspicion we would be totally isolated. I said that he had been watching too many disaster movies and that his attitude was a typically male one. I pointed out that in all the time I had been doing my foraging not one person had come anywhere near me. Nobody had threatened me. Nobody had interfered with me. The only people I had seen had all been looking rather nervous and just quietly going about their business as I was going about mine. Far from wanting to attack each other we had all tended to take avoiding action. I hadn't seen any signs of gang warfare.

Shahid said that this would come. He said it was because society – what little was left of it – was still in a state of shock and hadn't yet had time to reorganise, but that when it did there would be warring factions and leaders and power struggles just like before. I said that this was very depressing and that it contradicted what he had said earlier, about maybe now people would grow up and start taking responsibility. Also, I didn't see that it was necessarily correct. Why shouldn't people organise to cooperate and share? Why did he automatically assume that there would be a replay of what had gone before?

Shahid said that what he had said earlier about people taking responsibility had been said in a moment of weakness, before he had had time to get his brain together. He said that there was no reason to suppose that good would come out of evil: society couldn't be expected to mature overnight just because there had been a catastrophe. In fact, probably just the opposite would happen. He said that when there were shortages people always fought and became aggressive.

I don't think this is necessarily true. I know it was what

happened *before*, because of society being so large and impersonal and everyone feeling helpless on account of others being in control and pushing them around. But when it's only small groups and they're deciding for themselves the way to run their lives then it's different. Like I remember once when there was a bread shortage and Mum had some spare loaves in the freezer and she gave them to some of our neighbours that hadn't got any. She could have kept them all for us, but she didn't, in spite of not knowing when there was going to be any more bread on the shelves. Like, again, for instance, if Shahid and I had only one tin of food left between us we wouldn't fight each other for it, we'd share it. I told him this but he just said that I was naive and had an extraordinarily simplistic view of human nature.

Does that mean that he *would* fight me for it?

The eighth day. I asked Shahid if he remembered the time we'd played the survivors game with Mrs Dainty, when we were in our first year in Seniors. He said, 'No, what was that?' So then I reminded him – 'We had to write down what we'd save if the house were on fire' – and he said he did vaguely remember it. I asked him what he'd written and he thought about it and eventually said, 'The television set, probably.' I said, '*Television* set?' I couldn't believe anyone would risk their life just for a television set.

Shahid said, 'We'd just splashed out on a colour one. It was the family's most valuable possession.' I asked him what Mrs Dainty had had to say about it, but he couldn't remember.

The ninth day. This morning I said to Shahid that if we were going to go to Barnet we ought to make a list of things to take with us. He said, 'Yes, all right,' without sounding the least bit enthusiastic. I said, 'Well, are we going to go to Barnet or not?'

There is a terrible temptation just to stay where we are,

and yet I know that we can't. Sooner or later the food supplies will run out, and also there will be the danger of things like typhoid and cholera because of the water being polluted. And I suppose there just *might* be gangs. And already there are rats. I have seen them, big grey sewer rats running along the gutters. The other day I saw one in the window of a shop. It is only a question of time before they start coming in here. And in spite of sometimes seeming cosy, the reality is that this place is a tip, which means that the temptation to stay is actually nothing more than a cowardly fear of going somewhere else. But I wouldn't have thought Shahid would have had that fear, especially as the place we are going to is his brother's.

I asked him again, later on, 'Look, are we going to go or aren't we?' and he said, 'Yes, of course we are,' sounding quite irritable about it.

I don't know what his problem is. But anyway, we can't go until he is strong enough.

The tenth day. Last night, at about two o'clock, we were woken by a series of very loud explosions. I have never been so terrified in my life before, and I think Shahid was quite scared as well because even after they had stopped (they went on for about ten minutes) he didn't suggest going out to look. Instead we huddled together thinking our last hour had come. I know it is absolutely pathetic, but I really thought it was someone dropping nuclear bombs. When I confessed this to Shahid he didn't jeer as I expected he would but took it quite seriously and said it was the sort of thing a foreign government would do – not necessarily to take advantage of our being in a weak position but to kill off all the survivors and stop them spreading the infection. Then he thought about it and said darkly that it was the sort of thing any government would do. 'Including our own,' I said; to which Shahid said, 'You'd better believe it.'

(Dad would have called Shahid a member of the Loony

Left, but the more I think about things, in ways I never thought about them before, the more I begin to realise that nothing was as simple and clear-cut as Dad liked to pretend.)

Anyway, it wasn't a bomb, thank heavens, at least we don't think it was. We went outside this morning to look – because as Shahid said, if it *was* nuclear and there was radiation then we'd have had it by now in any case – and in the distance we could see fires raging. For the first time we explored the rest of this building, above the shop. There is a door in the side, like in Harry's old place, and Shahid managed to break the lock by using a hammer and chisel that was under the sink. We went inside and up the stairs and found a flat, very dark and depressing, just the sort of place, I should think, where the owner of this shop might have lived. It smelt foul, though not the sort of foul that means someone has died, more like a mixture of damp and stale frying and *urine*. There wasn't anybody there at all, but there was a skylight on to the roof which we were able to climb through and from there we could see right across to where the fires were. It was somewhere to the east, but I don't know how far away. Shahid said it looked as though a factory had gone up and that there had probably been a gas explosion.

He said, 'Of course, this sort of thing is going to happen more and more.' I said, 'Yes, and for all we know it could be pumping out toxic waste.'

This has finally made up our minds for us: we are going to go to Barnet.

The eleventh day. I wonder if Mum can have had any idea, when she told me to be happy, just what sort of things we were going to have to live through? I try not to give way, because I think if one ever actually *admitted* to oneself that it is like a nightmare then one would just dissolve into madness and hysteria, and besides, I wouldn't want Mum to know. It would worry her terribly.

For her sake I have to put a brave face on things and just

take each day as it comes. That means not looking back to what has gone before, nor speculating on what may be yet to come; in other words, living in a *vacuum*. But it is the only way.

Today Shahid practised walking, ready for Barnet. We walked all the way down the Edgware Road, to Marble Arch and back. At the entrance to an underground car park we saw some people. Actually there were only about half a dozen of them, but all in a group like that made me feel nervous. Especially as they were all *youths*. Shahid said, 'There you are, you see . . . it's starting.' I don't know why a small group of young men should make one feel under threat, but I was very glad when we were out of sight.

At Marble Arch I thought of Harry, and her party. Shahid obviously had the same thoughts, for he said, 'Do you want go down to Trafalgar Square and look for her?' For a moment I was tempted, but it is over a fortnight now. Even if the party had still been going on when she arrived, it surely wouldn't still be going on now? And even if it were, the chances of Harry being there must be remote.

I said to Shahid, 'It's too far for you to walk on your first day.' 'I can walk that far,' he said. I said, 'Maybe tomorrow.'

It isn't fair making Shahid my excuse. The plain truth is that I was too scared to go and look for Harry (I wouldn't be scared to speak to the thin girl that I see, but I would be scared to find Trafalgar Square still full of burning cars and people leaping about in the flames. They must all have been drunk or on drugs, or both), just as Shahid, for some reason I can't understand, is scared to call his brother. Well, not scared so much as reluctant, perhaps, is a better word. He tried another call box today, but only because I pushed him. He said he couldn't get through. I don't know whether to believe him or not.

The twelfth day. It has happened: a rat has got in. I opened the door into the shop and there it was, on the counter. I screamed so loudly that it took off, but Shahid says that is it, we are not staying here a minute longer. He says that he is quite strong enough to walk the few miles to Barnet and never mind bothering about another rucksack we will just fill the one that we have and *go*.

I am just going to write a note to Harry before we leave. I am going to tell her where she can find us and pin it to the door; just in case.

13

And when she got there
The cupboard was bare . . .
Yes, sir! Very bare.
Just as bare as a cupboard could be.
As bare as
bare
as bare
could be . . .
'Oh, Shahid,' whispered Fran.

He squatted, and picked up a handful of ash, letting it slowly trickle through his fingers.

To tell the truth, we have all our windows boarded up . . . first the Taj, now Siddiki's. *These people are like beasts . . .*

'Shahid?' Fran touched, timidly, at his arm.

He straightened up. 'I've done it again, haven't I?' He said it somewhat bitterly. Could he never get anything right? 'All this time,' he said. 'All this time that we've been waiting – '

'You weren't to know!'

'I might have guessed. You're supposed to be the one who thinks well of the human race, not me.'

Quickly she said, 'It can't have happened that long ago. The ashes are still warm. And that time when you rang – '

'Which time when I rang?' He prodded with the toe of his trainer at a blackened lump of timber. 'I couldn't get through when I rang. The line was dead. I told you.'

'No, I mean that other time . . . that night.'

He looked at her, frowning. 'What night?'

'The night of the storm,' said Fran.

The night of the storm ... he had rung Rahim on the night of the storm?

'The night before you got ill. You used the telephone in the shop.' She was studying him anxiously, scanning his face for at least some sign of recognition. 'You rang him to say we were on our way. Don't you remember?'

Slowly, he shook his head.

'Don't you remember anything?'

'I remember ... breaking the window.' With a tin of luncheon meat. He remembered that. 'I remember Harriet – being worried. In case someone got in.'

'You barricaded us.'

'Yes.' He nodded. That he remembered.

'Nothing else?'

'I remember the two of you ... something about ... the north pole. Some game – '

'That's right! We used to play at it, under the blankets.'

'I remember you talking about it.'

And then he had tried talking to them about submarines in the bath and they hadn't been interested. They hadn't wanted to know. They had frozen him out and he had felt hurt. And yet –

'That was when we'd settled down,' said Fran. 'That was after you'd telephoned.'

There had been some reason why he had felt it only right that he should be excluded. Something he had done, something he had not told them ... something –

White whores!

The words suddenly exploded in his head.

Have you taken leave of your senses? My father hardly cold in his grave and you want to do this to him? Defile his memory by carting your trash along with you? Is there no end to the disgrace you intend bringing on this family? You were lucky you weren't disowned long since! Going out with WHITE WHORES ... you try bringing them here and you'll all be sent packing, and that includes you! I'm warning you ... you bring them here –

Shahid put his hands to his forehead, pressing the tips of

his fingers hard into his temples, trying to drown out the memory of Rahim's voice, screaming its obscenities. *You and your whores! Your white whores!*

He became aware that Fran was touching him again; urgently laying her hand on his arm. 'Shahid? They might still be alive . . . we could ask.'

'Ask who?'

She looked around. The road was deserted: fields on one side, scrubland on the other.

'Down there.' She pointed ahead, to a side turning. 'They might be in one of the houses.'

He shook his head; vehement. 'No point!'

'We could try.'

'No point! No point!' At least if he could have offered her food and shelter it would have been some kind of repayment. As it was –

'Shahid! Don't give in . . . please!' Fran's arms tightened round him. 'Don't lose heart . . . not now! I couldn't bear it. After all we've been through . . . please, Shahid! Please!'

He struggled, for her sake, to pull together the shattered fragments of his self-esteem; to salvage some sense of purpose, however minor, from out of the ruins.

'So where do we go from here?' he said. (And, he might have added, to what end?)

'We'll go to Cornwall.'

Fran hooked her hair back. Her face, upturned to his, was strong and determined. Her features had lost the heavy, rather puddingish look they used to have. No one now could have accused her, as he remembered Julie once doing, of being 'fat and bovine'. (Julie, although pretty, hadn't really been the most charitable of persons; but then neither, looking back, had he. He was the one who had glibly dismissed Harriet as neurotic. She *had* been neurotic, but in the end she had had strength enough to go off by herself. It was more than he had had.)

'Do you agree? Shahid! Do you agree? We'll go to Cornwall?'

'If that's what you want,' he said.

146

He wondered how she thought they were going to get there. It was obvious madness. It would take them weeks.

'It's just over two hunded miles,' said Fran. A mere nothing.

'I've worked it out . . . if we can do an average of, say, twenty miles a day we'll be there in ten or twelve days. That's not counting today. Today I think we should just concentrate on getting out of London.'

Today they should just concentrate on getting out of London . . . past the road blocks. Past the soldiers. Past the guns.

'How?' he said, bluntly.

'I don't know. But there's got to be a way. They can't have sealed off every *single* exit.'

'They can, quite easily, if they've mobilised the army.'

'But I found a way in!'

'They probably weren't so worried about people getting in.'

'So I could have got out again the same way.'

'You don't know that. You didn't *get* out.'

'Well, I'm going to this time!' she cried. 'And so are you! So there!'

He pulled a face.

'Shall I tell you something?' said Fran. 'Shall I tell you what my mum said? She said, we have all our tomorrows still to come. And it's true! They're all there ahead of us – and we're going to live to see them. Because we're survivors! We've already proved it – in spite of colour televisions and pianos!'

He looked at her, puzzled.

'That was a *joke*,' said Fran.

'Oh.' He smiled, uncertainly; not getting it.

'I thought when people made jokes, people were supposed to laugh . . . you'd think,' she said, 'that you could make a little bit of an effort. You could at least *pretend* to be amused.'

He grinned, sheepishly. 'That's better,' she said. 'Now let's decide which way to go.'

He would have thought, since they didn't have a map, that deciding which way to go might be considered somewhat academic. Not so.

'We have to go west,' said Fran. 'So long as we keep going west, we'll be all right.'

They set off, along the Barnet Road.

'You are quite sure this is west?' she said.

He knew that it was. Somewhere out there were the film studios, which he had always wanted to visit. He had thought, at one time, that he might quite like to be in films — as a director, or course, not an actor. He had been foolish enough to confide this to Rahim, on the first occasion they had visited him, hoping Rahim might offer to drive him over to Elstree to have a look. All Rahim had said was, 'More of your stupid big-headed ideas!'

It was true, he did have stupid ideas. Coming to Barnet had been a stupid idea. He suddenly perceived, what should have been clear all along, that Rahim had never wanted him there. Fran and Harriet had merely been the scapegoats. He wondered if his brother had ever gone so far as to hope he would actually die, along with the rest of the family.

'I wish you'd talk to me,' said Fran.

He looked at her, bleakly. What was there, any more, to talk about?

'You didn't believe me,' she said, 'did you? When I said that we were survivors. You didn't believe me . . . well, we are. And I'll tell you how I know. I know because when you were sick I made a pact . . . if you died, then it meant that I would die, too. But if you got better, then it meant we were both going to live . . . we're going to come through this time and be a part of whatever comes after. Whatever *does* come after. Whether it's something good or something bad, we're going to be here to see it. Both of us. Together. That is something that I know.'

He was silent.

'You still don't believe me, do you?' she said.

He wanted to believe her. With one small, stubborn,

148

secret part of himself he wanted to. The rest of him had given up; just shrugged its shoulders and didn't care. It wasn't a question of believing or not believing, simply a question of going along with her.

'What can I do to convince you?' she said.

'You can't do anything. I was never into all that religious stuff.'

'I'm not asking you to be religious!'

'You're just asking me to have blind faith.'

'No,' she said. She slipped her arm through his and squeezed. 'I'm asking you to have the will to go on . . . to believe that there is some point in going on. To believe that it is *possible* to go on. And that we are *going* to go on. That's all.'

'You don't ask much,' he said.

'So what can I do?'

'You can tell me how we're going to get through that lot, for a start!'

They had rounded a slight bend in the road. Ahead of them, about a hundred metres away, was an army Land Rover, parked sideways on. A soldier was sitting in the driving seat. They could see him quite clearly, see the glint of his rifle in the sun. Across the road was a white pole, supported on trestles.

'Well?' said Shahid. 'What do we do?'

'Just keep on walking.'

'You want to get us shot?'

'I don't see why he should shoot us . . . we're not armed.'

'It's his job,' said Shahid. 'That's what he's there for.'

'To shoot people?'

'To stop people getting out.'

'He'll say something first.'

'Yeah, like, "Bang bang you're dead."'

'Well, what do you care?' She turned on him. 'You don't believe we're survivors anyway! If you're scared, stay there. *I*'ll go.'

She set off, back straight, head held high, towards the barrier. He moved swiftly to catch up with her.

149

'I mean it,' she said. 'You don't have to.'

'If you're going,' he said, 'then so am I. I don't want to be left on my own . . . I mean it,' he said. 'That's the truth.'

Together, shoulders touching, they moved forward.

'If he shouts stop,' said Shahid, 'stop.'

Nobody shouted stop. Nobody challenged them, nobody questioned them. They skirted the barrier, walked on down the road. After a bit, in unspoken agreement, they broke into a run. They ran until they could run no more.

'We made it!' Fran gasped, doubled over, triumphant, clutching at her side. 'I knew he wouldn't shoot us!'

The reason he hadn't shot them was that he was dead.

She thrust her hair back. 'You see? I said we'd find a way!'

Shahid bowed his head; not contradicting her.

'What's the matter? You don't seem to understand . . . *he let us through!* I told you! I said we were survivors!' Fran laughed, exultantly. 'Now perhaps you'll believe me!'

How could he not? He took her hand.

'Come on,' he said. 'Let's go to Cornwall.'

Jean Ure

AFTER THE PLAGUE

100 years after a Plague has devastated the planet, the great-grandson of two survivors travels from Cornwall to Croydon in search of the diary that his great-grandmother, Frances Latimer, had kept. But before he finds the diary, he falls and is knocked unconscious. When he wakes it is to see two women, April and Meta, staring at him as if they have never seen a man before . . .

Daniel finds that April and Meta's community has evolved very differently from his own. It is a place where power is in the hands of women and male aggression has been eliminated.

But which society is right? Which is more humane? April finds she is forced to choose . . .

Originally published as *Come Lucky April*, this is the sequel to *Plague*, winner of the Lancashire Book Award.

Jean Ure

WATCHERS AT THE SHRINE

'Hal, if you stay on here, you know perfectly well what will happen to you.'

'Yes! The same as'll happen to all the others. Why do I have to be different?' -

Hal's mother April has his best interests at heart when she and David send him away from the Croydon Community to avoid ritual castration. But now Hal is an outcast from his own community and is sent to live in Cornishtown, where the aggressive ways of the twentieth century survive 150 years after the plague struck.

Hal has to live with a family of Watchers, outdwellers with a religion that demands absolute obedience to the Power. On a journey to the shrine, Hal discovers a terrible truth – but where can he go to be safe?

This is the fascinating conclusion to the 'Plague' trilogy, begun in *Plague* and continued in *After the Plague* (originally published as *Come Lucky April*).

Cynthia D Grant

MARY WOLF

*We hurl along the ribbon of highway 1, tires
screeching on the curves, almost flying. Beside me,
my father is making sounds like an animal caught in
the jaws of a trap. Far below us, the restless ocean
glitters like the fan of silver water he jumped
through to please me, a lifetime ago. We laughed so
hard. Now he's someone I don't know. He's like one
of those animals you see on the road, that's been
run over so many times you can't even tell what it
was.*

When Mary's father loses his job, life changes for
the whole family. As the weeks turn into months,
Mr Wolf becomes even more volatile and a
catastrophe seems almost inevitable . . .

"Grant establishes the desperation of lives ruled by
nightmare, drawing the threads of her narrative ever
tighter so that only extraordinary force can alter her
characters' destinies."

Publishers Weekly